The Royal Ballet School Diaries

Naomi's
new step

Naomi gave them all a weak smile. She looked tired, and a little red-eyed, Ellie thought. Ellie watched Naomi go out of the dorm to see her parents off. She noticed that Naomi was hugging her mum for what seemed like a long time. It made her think back to the first time she'd met Naomi, when Naomi had all but shooed her parents out of the dorm, she was so anxious to start her own life at The Royal Ballet School.

Something was wrong with Naomi, Ellie could tell. But what?

Look out for more stories from The Royal Ballet School:

The Royal Ballet School Diaries

Naomi's new step

Alexandra Moss

■SCHOLASTIC

To Darcey and Ella Haddow,
my gorgeous goddaughters

Special thanks to Sue Mongredien

Scholastic Children's Books,
Commonwealth House, 1-19 New Oxford Street,
London, WC1A 1NU, UK
a division of Scholastic Ltd
London ~ New York ~ Toronto ~ Sydney ~ Auckland
Mexico City ~ New Delhi ~ Hong Kong

Published in the UK by Scholastic Ltd, 2005
Series created by Working Partners Ltd

ISBN 0 439 95970 5

Printed by Nørhaven Paperback A/S, Denmark

2 4 6 8 10 9 7 5 3 1

Prologue

Dear Diary,

Hooray!!!

I've passed my Year 7 appraisal! So now it's official: my place at The Royal Ballet School is safe for another year. What a <u>huge</u> relief! I was so nervous when the letter arrived with my results I could hardly bring myself to look at Mum's face as she read it. But then she smiled and handed me the letter to read for myself.

Now that I've seen the good news in black and white, I'm just sooooo happy! It feels like all my hard work last term has paid off.

Mum was as excited as I was — she scanned the letter into the computer and e-mailed it to Grandma in Chicago. She's pinned up a copy on her office wall, too! We had a celebratory dinner with Phoebe and Bethany yesterday.

I spoke to Grace on the phone. She passed, too! And Belle sent me a text message from the London hotel she's staying in with her mum, to say she'd passed as well. No surprises there, of course. Belle seems to be awesome at just about everything.

Belle came to stay here in Oxford over half-term, because her mum was too busy to have her — but then halfway through the week, her mum called out of the blue with news that she had a job interview in London, and could spend time with Belle after all. So Belle rushed off down to London the day before we all received our assessment results.

Belle and her mum seem to have a difficult

relationship sometimes, but she was still so excited about seeing her during the vacation.

The apartment sure is quieter now Belle's left, especially after we tried to make crêpes and accidentally set off the fire alarm! The more I get to know Belle the more I like her. I was sorry to see her go, but I was glad to have some quality time with my <u>own</u> mum — and Steve. Or should I say, my new stepdad! It still feels strange saying that!

No news from the other girls yet, but I guess I'll find out how they've done soon enough. It's back to The Royal Ballet School tomorrow for the second half of spring term: back to ballet classes, the beautiful White Lodge, and all my friends. I can't wait!

Chapter One

"Ellie! You're back!"

"Hey, Grace!" Ellie Brown threw her arms around her friend Grace in the Year 7 girls' dormitory and hugged her. It felt so good to be back at The Royal Ballet School after half-term. As much as she loved spending time in Oxford with her mum and stepdad, Steve, Ellie was always eager to get back to school and her daily ballet classes – not to mention her school friends, who loved ballet as much as she did.

Ellie glanced around the long, curving dorm room where all twelve of the Year 7 girls slept. At the far end, Kate, Megan and Rebecca had also arrived and were unpacking. Ellie waved hello to them.

Grace went and sat cross-legged on her bed, then looked expectantly at Ellie. "So . . ." she began, "time for the million-dollar question. . . Have you heard how the others did in their appraisals?"

"Only Belle," Ellie replied, as she heaved her case on to her bed and unzipped it. "She passed – of course!"

Ellie and Grace both chuckled. Half-French Belle Armand was a good friend now, but at first everybody had thought she was stuck-up and arrogant. In time, however, Ellie had found out that Belle's stand-offishness was because her parents were in the middle of a bitter separation.

Belle hadn't wanted to leave the life she had known with both parents in Paris to come and live in England, and her mum kept changing her mind about where she wanted to make her new home. So Belle hadn't made any effort to make new friends at The Royal Ballet School in case she had to move again.

But, almost in spite of herself, Belle had come to enjoy being at The Royal Ballet School, and luckily it now seemed she was here to stay.

Kate and Megan both wandered over to give Ellie a hug, and confirm that all had gone well with their own appraisals.

"A huge weight off my mind," sighed Kate. "It's so great to be back!"

Ellie nodded in agreement.

As the two girls went back to the other side of the dorm, Ellie opened her suitcase to start putting her clothes away but then changed her mind. Unpacking could wait. She was far more interested in getting all Grace's news! She went and sat next to Grace on her bed. "So, what did your mum say when she opened your letter saying you'd passed?" she asked eagerly, kicking off her trainers and settling comfortably on to her bed.

Grace made a face. Then she glanced around

as if checking that nobody else was listening and said, "Don't tell anyone, but she actually phoned up the school to find out who was the top in our year! She wanted to find out if it was me. I was *soooo* embarrassed."

Ellie's mouth fell open in surprise, and then she closed it again hurriedly. Grace's mum sure was competitive. "Gee. . . Um. . . What did they say?" she asked. "*Were* you top?"

Grace shrugged again. "I don't know," she replied. "They wouldn't tell Mum anything specific. I think all the marks are confidential."

"Well, I guess all that really matters is whether you get to stay or not," Ellie said.

Grace nodded. But she didn't seem too convinced. Still, Ellie was glad that Grace felt able to confide in her.

She nudged her friend gently and struggled to think of the right words. "Well, I bet you did awesomely. Better than me. Should I call your mum and tell her so?"

Finally, Grace giggled. "Don't you dare!" she said, sounding a bit more cheerful. Then her eyes clouded again. "You won't tell any of the others about Mum calling the school, will you?" she asked anxiously.

Ellie shook her head and put an arm around Grace's shoulder. "I'll take it to the grave," she said seriously.

"Take what to the grave?" came a familiar lilting Irish accent. "You sound awful serious over there, Ellie Brown!"

Ellie and Grace both spun around to see their friend Lara coming into the dorm.

Ellie jumped up and hugged Lara. "How was your vacation? I've been trying to call you for ever!" she cried.

Lara laughed and slung her bags on to her bed, which was on the other side of Ellie's. "We were staying with my auntie all week, in the middle of deepest darkest, *rainiest* nowhere, so my phone had no reception," she explained.

"I wasn't ignoring your calls – honest! There were times when I would have sold my sister for a good old natter with you on the phone!"

"That's OK, then. You're forgiven," Ellie said, grinning. "How are you anyway? And how was your appraisal?"

"Fine and fine," Lara replied, untying her long red hair from its ponytail and shaking it loose over her shoulders. "How about you two?"

As the three of them discussed their appraisals, the door opened again and Bryony walked in. "Hi, guys!" she called, and hugged each of the girls. "Well, how did we all do?"

After hearing from the others, Bryony told them happily that she had done well in the assessment too. But then a shadow passed over her face. "Kelly didn't, though," she added.

"Who's Kelly?" asked Kate, frowning in concern. Ellie remembered that Kelly was the Year 8 student who had been assigned as

Bryony's "guide". Each Year 7 student had a Year 8 guide to help sort out any problems he or she might have during the first year.

"She still passed though, didn't she?" asked Lara anxiously. Her usually sparkling green gaze was steady and serious. Ellie knew that Lara often chatted with Kelly in the common room shared by the Year 7 and 8 girls. They were from neighbouring Irish towns.

Bryony shook her head, her own eyes troubled. "No," she said in a low voice. "She's been assessed out."

Ellie sat down heavily on her bed. "No way!" she breathed. It was the unthinkable – not making the grade at The Royal Ballet School. Poor Kelly! "How totally awful," she added, shaking her head.

"I know," Bryony replied quietly.

Ellie glanced over at Grace. Although it was terrible news for Kelly, Ellie couldn't help hoping this bombshell might help put things in perspective for Grace's mum. Things could be far, far worse than not being top of the class.

Bryony unzipped one of her cases and pulled out the regulation pink leotard that all the Year 7 girls wore. She stroked it lovingly. "I really hope I never have to go through what Kelly's going through," she said. "But sometimes you can work and work, and just not be good enough."

Lara nodded seriously. "I know," she said. "That's the scary thing. Kelly did work *really* hard before her appraisal. I know she did. But..."

Ellie bit her lip. She knew what Lara was saying was true. There were no guarantees of making the grade in the dancing world, no matter how hard you tried, however hard you practised, however much you gave it your all. She shivered. "That *is* kind of scary," she agreed.

There was a moment's silence in the dorm,

then, thankfully, the door swung open and in came Belle, dragging a very full and very expensive suitcase behind her.

At the sight of the immaculately-groomed, dark-haired French girl, Ellie grinned as she remembered back to the start of the spring term when Belle had stalked into the dorm for the first time with her nose in the air and without a second glance at any of them. Thank goodness things had changed!

This time, Belle rushed around, kissing everybody on the cheek. "I am so glad to have escaped my mother," she confessed, rolling her eyes at them all. "That woman has driven me crazy!"

Ellie giggled. Belle and her mum still seemed to have a tempestuous relationship, to say the least! "Any news on your mum's job?" she asked.

Belle smoothed a hand through her long, dark hair and smiled. "Yes – she was offered the position!" she replied. "Although anybody wanting to employ my mother must be very brave, I think." She grinned. "So we have been driving all over London, looking for somewhere for her to live. Buckingham Palace was not up for rent, unfortunately, but we found a house quite near London, which *Maman* will be moving to next week." She rolled her eyes again comically. "Do you know, after all our arguing, I am starting to wish she was back in Paris already!"

The other girls giggled. "I can't wait to meet your mum," Lara chuckled. "When is she going to come and visit?"

Belle looked horrified at the thought. "Never, I hope!" she cried. Then she lowered her voice. "She was very excited about coming to the school today but I wouldn't let her in the door. I told her she had to say goodbye to me in the car park. I said that parents weren't allowed inside the building!"

"Belle!" Ellie snorted, chuckling at the thought of Belle bossing her mum around.

"That seems a bit harsh," Bryony added, laughing too.

Belle put her head on one side and pouted. "I do not think so," she replied. "My *maman*, she is too. . . What is the right word? She is too over the top. Too much!" She shook her head. "No, The Royal Ballet School is *my* place. Not hers. She is banned!"

Ellie smiled. To think that Belle had been so sullen and unfriendly last term! It was almost like having a different person in the dorm — a vivacious, chatty, bubbly Belle, who seemed a million miles from the rude and seemingly arrogant girl they'd first met.

"Now all we need is Naomi, and our gang is back together again," Lara said happily, hanging up her leotard and pink chiffon ballet skirt in her wardrobe. "Has anybody heard from her?"

"She's been in Blackpool the whole vacation with her grandmother," Ellie said. "I've sent her a few text messages but I haven't heard anything back from her."

"Ah, well. . ." Grace said affectionately. "Knowing our Naomi, she'll have got herself a job on Blackpool pier, doing people's horoscopes, and reading their palms. I can see it now – Madame Naomi Reveals Your Destiny!"

Ellie and the others burst out laughing at the thought of their astrology-crazy friend gazing mysteriously into a crystal ball.

Between giggles, Lara whisked her leotard out of the wardrobe again and draped it over her head, pulling the edges under her chin like a headscarf. "Cross my palm with silver, young man," she croaked, "and I will tell you your fortune!"

"Hey! Madame Naomi herself!" Bryony cried, beaming at Naomi as she entered the room with her parents.

"Yaaay!" the girls all cheered.

"We were just talking about you," Lara added, her leotard still hanging around her face.

Naomi gave them all a weak smile. She looked tired, and a little red-eyed, Ellie thought. Not her usual bouncy self at all. Maybe she'd had a lot of late nights. Probably making the most of no Royal Ballet School curfew while she was on holiday!

Ellie watched Naomi put her bags on her bed and then go out of the dorm to see her parents off. Ellie noticed that Naomi was hugging her mum for what seemed like a long time. It made her think back to the first time she'd met Naomi, when Naomi had all but shooed her parents out of the dorm, she was so anxious to start her own life at The Royal Ballet School.

Something was wrong with Naomi, Ellie could tell. But what?

Chapter Two

"Something's going on with Naomi," Lara said bluntly, echoing Ellie's thoughts.

Just then, Naomi came back into the dorm. She sat at the edge of her bed.

"Naomi . . . is everything all right?" Ellie asked softly.

"No. . ." Naomi admitted, her gaze firmly fixed on the floor. "Not really. . ." She heaved a sigh and then looked up. "It's not good," she said, forcing an unconvincing smile on to her face. "I didn't make it," she added hoarsely. "I've been appraised out. I'll be leaving The Royal Ballet School at the end of the year."

Ellie stared at Naomi in horror.

"This is a joke, right?" Kate said. "Naomi, say it's a joke!"

Naomi shook her head. "Afraid not."

Ellie was winded with shock. Sure, Naomi wasn't the most technically perfect student in ballet class. And OK, so she hadn't worked her socks off, like some of the other girls. But appraised out? She just couldn't believe it!

What was it the Year 8 girls had said about the likelihood of being appraised out in Year 7? *It's sooo not likely to happen. . .*

She rushed over and put her arms around Naomi. "I am so sorry to hear that, Naomi." Her voice wobbled on the words, and she felt her eyes fill up with tears.

"Oh, Naomi," Grace said miserably. "What awful news!"

"Can you appeal?" Bryony asked. "Can you ask to be appraised again?"

Naomi shook her head. "No," she told them. "The decision's made. I've got to go at the end of summer term – and that's that." She forced a smile. "I know, I know . . . I should have taken my boring foot exercises more seriously," she said wryly. "I never made a big deal of it, but . . . my parents were told when I was accepted here that I was a borderline case – that my feet might prove to be a problem if I didn't work hard to make them more flexible. Mum and Dad nagged me over the Christmas break to knuckle down when I got back to school. But you know what I'm like, always getting distracted. . ." Naomi sighed heavily. "So here I am on the scrapheap at eleven. Doomed!" she joked.

Nobody laughed. They all came over to hug her instead.

"We will miss you so much, Naomi," Belle said, her dark eyes full of emotion. "The school will be so quiet without you. Who is going to tell me my horoscope when you've gone? Who is going to make all the jokes?"

Naomi gave her a weak smile. "Oh, don't," she said. "I'll be blubbing again in a minute." She rubbed her eyes. "That's all I've been doing since I saw the wretched appraisal letter the other day – bawling my eyes out."

"Oh, Naomi. . ." Grace said, reaching out to squeeze Naomi's hand. "What will you do?" she asked tentatively.

Naomi gave another huge sigh. "I don't know yet," she said. "The school is being brilliant – really supportive. Miss Purvis and Ms Bell both phoned me up to talk about it, and Miss Purvis said that I'd have counselling sessions with her and Ms Bell this term, to discuss my options."

Ellie was relieved to hear that the Head of Lower School and the Lower School Ballet Principal would be advising her friend.

Naomi wearily pushed her hair out of her eyes. "Right now, though, I feel like I'm in a whirl," she added. "I can't make any decisions. I don't know what I'm going to do."

She bit her lip and stared down at her feet. "The worst thing is, I feel like I've really let my family down," she confessed in a low voice. "I mean, they've spent a fortune on ballet lessons for me over the years, and now I've thrown it all away." Her shoulders seemed to slump even further downwards. "I've blown it, haven't I? I have totally blown it."

"You haven't!" Ellie protested indignantly. "You got your place here at The Royal Ballet School fair and square. You didn't blow it! It's amazing to get here at all. Think of all those thousands of girls who apply every year, and *you* were picked. Nobody can take that away from you, Naomi. And your parents will always be proud of you for getting so far."

"Ellie's right," Lara said, patting Naomi on the shoulder. "You haven't let anybody down. We were just talking about Kelly before you came in. You know Kelly McGovern in

Year 8, Bryony's guide? Well, she's been appraised out, too. And it's nothing to do with how hard she worked, or anything. It's like. . . She went as far as she could. Nobody thinks any less of her. It's just really sad."

"It *is* really sad," Naomi agreed. A tear rolled down her cheek and she quickly dashed it away. "That's the worst bit – how sad I feel at the thought of leaving. Saying goodbye to you lot, knowing that you'll all be carrying on without me." Another tear plopped down on to her knee.

"Oh, Naomi, don't cry, please," Ellie said, passing her a tissue and on the verge of tears herself again. This was just so unbelievably awful!

Naomi blew her nose and gave them all a watery smile. "You know, you'd all better become famous ballerinas for *my* sake now," she said, her voice still shaky. "If I can't boast about my own ballet triumphs, it'll be something, at least, being able to brag about my superstar friends!"

Ellie tried to laugh, to make Naomi feel better, but it came out as a little sob.

"And *we'll* all be saying how proud we are to know Naomi Crawford, ace astrologer," said Grace.

"And brilliant singer," added Lara.

"And hilarious comedian," put in Kate.

"And wonderful friend," Ellie said, as she held tight to Naomi's hand.

The bell rang just then, making everybody jump.

"Lunchtime already?" Belle said, frowning down at her watch. "I had forgotten how fast time goes in this place."

Naomi got to her feet. "I'd better go and wash my face," she said. "Will somebody wait for me? I don't feel like walking in there on my own today."

While they all waited for Naomi to go and

splash some cold water on her face in the girls' bathroom, Ellie sat down on her bed. She was still reeling from the shock of her friend's awful news. She remembered the rush of relief she'd felt on reading her own appraisal letter, and tried to imagine the horrible gut-wrenching Naomi must have felt at the arrival of *hers*. How many times would you have to read something like that before the reality finally sank in? She could hardly bear to think about Naomi scanning the letter repeatedly, hoping her eyes were tricking her, hoping she'd made a mistake, or that there was some terrible typing error.

"Are you all right, Ellie?" Grace asked in a subdued voice.

"Kind of," Ellie replied. "But it's like . . . nothing's going to be the same now."

"I know what you mean," Lara sighed.

Naomi came back just then. "Well, at least my days of soggy school quiche are numbered," she told them, and tried to smile. "But, you know what?" she sighed. "I'd eat soggy school quiche every day for the next five years if it meant staying here."

Ellie slipped an arm through Naomi's. "Come on," she said quietly. "Let's go and enjoy that soggy quiche together while we can."

Dear Diary,

I feel blown away by Naomi's news. I keep half-forgetting about it, and then WHAM! I get hit by the shock of it all over again, and I just feel sick. It's so horrible. I am so, so sad. I can't imagine life here without Naomi. The dorm just won't be the same without her.

She seems pretty low – which isn't surprising. It is truly terrible seeing her cry when usually she's so upbeat about everything. We've all been in floods of tears with her.

Right now, she says she can't think about anything other than the fact that she's leaving. I just hope that once she gets over the bad news, she'll be able to make the most of the rest of her time here with us.

The dorm is a pretty quiet place tonight. Usually, everybody's noisy and excited on the first night back at school, but I guess we all feel so shell-shocked by the news that nobody feels like doing anything much.

Mrs Hall came in to see us all, and gave Naomi the biggest hug. She was really nice about the whole thing, saying that Naomi leaving is such sad news for everybody in Year 7, and that whenever any of us feel upset about it, we can go and talk to her about it if we want to.

None of us guessed that Naomi was a borderline case... It's hard not to think of her as a star in the making! What will she do now?

Chapter Three

Ellie woke up the next morning with the usual feeling of excitement in her stomach. Monday morning and her first ballet class of the week! She still had to pinch herself sometimes, she felt so lucky. At The Royal Ballet School, students had a ballet class every day – Ellie's idea of heaven!

She rolled over in bed, to make some happy comment about it to Grace. In the dim morning light that was just creeping under the curtains, she caught sight of Naomi, in her bed on the other side of Grace, wide awake and staring at the ceiling.

The sight of Naomi's pale, miserable face stopped the words in Ellie's throat, and she was overwhelmed with sadness as she suddenly remembered what had happened.

Of all the girls in the dorm, Naomi was usually the one who had to be dragged kicking and screaming from her sleep. She was the first to admit that she would never be a "morning person". Ellie had never even known her to be awake before Mrs Hall, their housemother, came in and snapped the lights on with her usual cheery, "Good morning, girls, rise and shine!" Yet today, there she was, looking as if she'd barely slept a wink. *And she probably hasn't. . .* Ellie thought to herself. How could anyone sleep when they had their whole future to work out?

Ellie swung her legs out of bed. "Morning, Naomi," she said quietly. "You OK?"

Naomi plastered a big grin on her face, but her eyes didn't sparkle in their usual way, and Ellie knew she was faking it.

"Sure," Naomi replied. "Just wondering if

that spider is about to drop on Grace's head."

Grace sat bolt upright. "What spider? Where?" she screeched, waking Bryony and Belle, who both pulled their covers over their heads.

Naomi chuckled. "Sorry, Grace," she said. "There isn't really a spider. But I couldn't resist."

Grace fell back against her pillow, still casting furtive looks up at the ceiling. "You'll regret that, Naomi Crawford," she grumbled.

Mrs Hall chose that moment to pop her head around the door. "Good morning, g—!" she said, and then stopped in surprise as she realized so many of them were already awake. She put the lights on and peered around. "Where are my Year 7 girls?" she joked. "Who are these strangers in their beds who are actually awake at seven o'clock in the morning?"

There was a groan from Lara's bed. "Is it really seven o'clock?" she moaned in a muffled voice.

Mrs Hall laughed. "Ah well, I see I've still got my Lara in there," she said. "But the rest of you – well! You never fail to surprise me!"

Naomi put her feet into her slippers and wrapped her dressing gown around herself as Mrs Hall left the dorm. "You know, in a bizarre kind of way, I'm even going to miss Mrs Hall waking me up every morning," she said. "What am I going to do without my daily 'Good morning, girls, rise and shine!'" Her high-pitched, cheery tone was a perfect impression of their housemother's breezy wake-up call and a couple of the girls giggled, but it just made Ellie feel a bittersweet pang of sadness.

"Don't worry, I can phone you at seven every morning, and wake you up, if you miss it that much," Grace joked, sticking her tongue out at Naomi. "Payback for the non-existent spider."

"And then I'll phone ten minutes later,

saying, 'Naomi Crawford, are you *still* not dressed?'" Lara added, finally sitting up and rubbing the sleep out of her eyes. "We'll give you a week and see how much you miss Mrs Hall then."

Naomi yawned and stretched her arms above her head. "A week? You'll have forgotten all about me by then," she said, with a pout. "You'll be saying, 'What *was* the name of that other girl in our year? You know, the one who was chucked out at the end of summer term because she was so rubbish?'"

"We will *not*!" said Grace fiercely, grabbing her towel and washbag. "Naomi, don't say such awful things!"

Ellie watched Grace march off to the bathroom. It was unlike gentle Grace to ever raise her voice, but Ellie knew exactly why she had this time – because Naomi's jokey remark was so far away from how everybody felt. None of them would ever be able to forget Naomi –

which would make being without her that much harder. Ellie sighed as she picked up her own towel and headed off to shower.

Maybe joking about it is the easiest way for Naomi to handle the crisis right now, Ellie thought to herself as she shampooed her hair with more vigour than usual. *Naomi's got to get through this in her own way. We just have to let her do that, and support her all we can.* Ellie sighed again, glad that nobody could see her mournful expression. This half of term was turning out to be emotionally exhausting already, and it hadn't even really started yet.

"Good morning, everybody!" called Ms Wells, as Ellie and the rest of the Year 7 girls walked into their first ballet class of the second half of term. Ms Wells's eyes alighted briefly on Naomi, and her face softened. "How are we all?" she asked.

"Glad to be back, *mademoiselle*," Belle said

straight away, dropping a beautiful curtsey.

"Glad to hear it, Belle," Ms Wells replied.

Ellie saw there was a twinkle in their teacher's eye as she spoke to her newest pupil. Belle and Ms Wells had started off with a few differences of opinion at the beginning of term – because Belle had been used to French-taught ballet techniques that differed from some of The Royal Ballet School's techniques. Belle needed a little prompting to get used to doing some things differently. But Belle had risen to the challenge and all that seemed behind them now.

Naomi was being unusually quiet, Ellie noticed, feeling another wrench of sadness. As a self-confessed show-off, Naomi loved to clown around. She could mimic her fellow students – and teachers – to perfection. Ellie had been weak with laughter at Naomi's antics more times than she could remember. This morning, however, Naomi's eyes seemed far away and, while she performed all the movements diligently, Ellie could tell that her friend's heart wasn't in it today.

Ellie couldn't imagine how hard it must be for Naomi to be here in ballet class, with her failed appraisal still raw and painful, knowing she'd been judged as a dancer who wasn't up to scratch.

As Ellie watched a pale, drawn Naomi stretch out her muscles at the end of the class, it felt almost as if Mrs Hall's joke that morning had come true – Naomi looked so sad, it was as though an impostor really *had* taken the place of Ellie's larger-than-life friend.

Thankfully, after ballet class was over, Naomi seemed to cheer up a little. In fact, Ellie realized, as the girls were sitting down in maths class later that morning, flashes of the old Naomi were definitely reappearing.

"Oliver Stafford, I do declare! A blind

man's cut off all your hair," Naomi teased, fluffing up Oliver's short, spiky new haircut.

Ellie giggled at the flush spreading over Oliver's cheeks. He was so vain, it did him good to be teased occasionally.

"At least I'm not a reject like you, Naomi Crawford," Oliver replied coldly. "How much longer do we have to put up with you? Just another few months, isn't it?"

Naomi gasped as if she'd been slapped across the face. She swung away from Oliver at once and sat down, pulling out her maths books with trembling fingers.

Ellie's amusement at Naomi's good-natured teasing drained away on hearing Oliver's cruel response. "Don't you dare speak to Naomi like that!" Ellie said hotly, her heart pounding furiously in her chest.

"Yeah, just you mind your nasty mouth, Oliver Stafford!" shouted Lara.

"I wish they'd chuck *you* out," added Grace,

glaring at Oliver as she put a protective arm around Naomi.

Before Oliver could reply, Mr Best, their maths teacher, strolled into the room. "What's all the shouting about?" he asked mildly. "I could hear you lot all the way down the corridor. Don't tell me you're discussing *mathematics* with such passion and excitement?"

The class fell silent. A few people shot glares at Oliver, Ellie included. As usual, he didn't own up to being the cause of the shouting.

Mr Best looked expectantly around the room. "Nobody's going to fill me in? Shame," he said. "As a mathematician, I hate unsolved mysteries." He clapped his hands briskly. "Never mind, let's look at a few equations together instead then. That will cheer me up no end! Page 47 of your textbooks, please!"

A groan went around the classroom, but

everyone obediently pulled out their maths books and turned to the right page.

Ellie glanced over at Naomi. "You OK?" she mouthed.

"Sure," Naomi replied, with a shaky little smile. "It'll take more than Hair-do Stafford to rattle my cage." She said the last sentence deliberately loudly so that the whole class heard. A few giggles started up.

"Hair-*don't*, you mean," said Lara, equally loudly. And Oliver's ears turned crimson.

Mr Best glanced from Naomi to Oliver but didn't pursue the issue. "So . . ." he continued, "all on page 47? Let's start thinking about the glories of algebra!"

Ellie soon found herself tangled up in the puzzling equations, and the lesson passed without further incident.

Afterwards, it was time for lunch, and she and Lara both linked arms protectively with Naomi as they went towards the dining room.

"I feel like the Queen with her convoy of bodyguards," Naomi joked, as Grace, Belle and Bryony followed behind. "Nobody will dare come near, with you guys guarding me."

"Too right they won't," Ellie said firmly as they came to a stop in front of the menu boards. "Oh, look, Naomi, it's your lucky day! Spinach quiche. Every queen's favourite lunch."

Naomi laughed and gently disentangled herself from her friends' arms to get a tray. "Seriously, guys ... I'm really touched," she said. "You all sticking up for me back in class like that. . ." She dropped a little curtsey to them. "You didn't have to do that."

"We know we didn't," said Lara, elbowing her jokily. "It was just an excuse to have a go at Hair-don't. Nothing to do with you, Naomi."

"Oh, well in that case. . ." said Naomi, pretending to be offended. Then she went back to being serious. "Thanks, though.

Everybody is being so nice to me. Well, all except for Oliver."

"Like he ever mattered anyway," said Grace loyally.

"Exactly," Naomi grinned, and for the first time since she'd been back, the smile reached her eyes as well as her mouth.

The six friends chose their lunches and sat down. Matt Haslum, one of the Year 7 boys, came over to join them. "Half the boys in our year have stopped speaking to Oliver," he told them. "What he said to Naomi this morning was well out of order."

"About time they saw the light and realized what we've known for ages. That the boy's an *eejit*," said Lara in her strongest Irish accent, biting into a forkful of quiche. "What took them so long?"

Naomi looked bemused. "They've stopped speaking to him because of what he said to *me*?" she asked.

"That's right," Matt replied.

Naomi began to laugh. "Guys, let's not make this into a big deal – not for my sake, anyway," she said. "I couldn't live with myself if he was found sobbing in the boys' dorm all because of a stupid remark he made to yours truly." She dug her fork into her quiche. "It would take me years of counselling to get over the guilt." She paused for dramatic effect, and then shrugged. "Well, a few minutes, at least!"

On Wednesday morning, after their usual ballet class, Ellie noticed that Naomi wasn't getting her history books ready for their next lesson, like everybody else was.

"Aren't you coming to class, Naomi?" she asked in surprise, stuffing her own pencil case and textbooks into a bag.

Naomi, who was sitting on her bed, gave Ellie a rueful smile. "I've got my first 'session' with Ms Bell now," she said in a funny voice, and made a face. "I think I'd actually rather do an hour of history with you guys, believe it or not."

"What do you think you'll talk about then?" Lara asked with interest.

Naomi yawned. "Blah, blah, blah, you failed, blah, blah, blah, go back to regular school, you loser," she said, scuffing her foot along the floor.

Ellie tutted. "Hey! Don't start that all over again!" she said. "I'm sure it won't be like that at all!"

"Nobody's going to be calling you a loser," Kate said quietly, but forcefully.

"And if they do, tell us where they live and we'll go round there and sort them out!" Lara said fiercely.

Naomi lay down on her bed, looking very much as if she wasn't going anywhere fast. "I can't see there's much point in me going any-way," she said. "I've got nothing to say to them, other than, 'I don't know what I'm going to do.' It's going to take all of five minutes."

Ellie went over and grabbed one of her hands to pull her up. "Come on," she said firmly. "Just go. I'm sure they'll help you figure it out. And you can tell us all about it over lunch."

Naomi got to her feet, still looking reluctant. "OK, OK," she said. "Here goes nothing, guys. See you all in the dining room."

After the history lesson, Ellie and the others made their way to the dining room for lunch.

Ellie held her breath as she saw Naomi come in and pick up a tray.

"How does she look to you?" she asked Grace.

"Not very happy," Grace replied bluntly, watching Naomi dithering at the pasta bar. "Oh, I was really hoping this meeting was going to cheer her up."

"We all were," Lara said, putting a bright smile on her face as Naomi came over to their table. "Hey, Naomi. How was your careers meeting? Did they have any exciting suggestions?"

Naomi shrugged.

"Well, what did they say?" Ellie prompted.

Naomi shrugged again. "Oh, you know, lots of options still open. . . You've got a bright future, et cetera, et cetera," she said, waving a hand airily. Then she glanced down at her Spaghetti Bolognese. "I think I just made a terrible mistake, choosing this today," she said. "I'm bound to spill the orange sauce down my nice white shirt. So, how was history?"

Ellie put another mouthful of her jacket potato into her mouth and chewed it thoughtfully. No prizes for guessing that Naomi wasn't in a hurry to talk about her careers meeting. She really hoped something would happen to cheer up her friend, and fast!

*   *   *

Later that afternoon, it was Year 7's weekly choreography class. "Hello, everybody," Ms Denton, their choreo teacher, said at the start of the lesson. "I've got an important announcement to make today."

Grace immediately put her hand up. "Is it about the choreo competition?" she asked eagerly.

Ms Denton laughed at the expectant light in Grace's eyes. "Goodness, you're keen," she joked. "Yes, Grace, I'm going to tell you a bit more about the Junior Choreography Competition today."

An excited buzz broke out around the room. Ellie already knew that Grace was keen on the idea of choreographing a piece for the annual competition. They'd all heard that the Year 7 students competed in a category with the Year 8s, and contestants had to prepare a short, original piece, a few minutes long.

Grace was obviously interested, and Ellie could see that Alice was listening intently to Ms Denton too, as were Matt and Nick.

"For anyone who doesn't know yet, this year's competition will be taking place just before the Easter holiday, in mid-April," Ms Denton went on. "If you are at all interested in choreographing a short piece, between two and three minutes long, on any theme at all, then please stay behind after today's class. I need to hand in a list of all competitors by Monday."

"What happens then, Ms Denton?" asked Naomi.

Ellie was surprised to hear Naomi asking the question. Naomi hadn't seemed very interested in anything lately. Maybe getting involved in the choreo competition would help her friend feel more like her old self again.

"Well, Naomi," Ms Denton replied, "then, the entrants need to assemble their dancers quickly – they only have until the third week of March to get pieces ready for the pre-selection process, where you'll be asked to perform your pieces in front of the Lower School Ballet Principal and the other dance teachers. You also need to prepare a document which details your proposed choreography, costumes, music and set. I can help you with that, so don't be too alarmed!" She smiled encouragingly at them and went on. "Several entrants will be knocked out of the competition at the pre-selection stage. For those who get through, it's more hard work for the following few weeks, polishing and perfecting your routine for the competition proper at the end of term."

"I'm definitely going in for it," Grace whispered to Ellie. "I can't wait!"

"And I'm excited to tell you," said Ms Denton with a glint in her eye, "that we will be having a celebrity judge for the competition itself – Jonathan Wright, the up-and-coming choreographer currently at Birmingham Royal Ballet."

A buzz went around the room. Ellie smiled at Grace and flexed her feet thoughtfully. Although she had no particular wish to choreograph anything herself, it would be kind of fun if she got picked to dance in somebody else's routine.

"Now then," Ms Denton said, over the excited chatter, "as I said, those of you who are interested, please stay behind after this class and I'll talk you through the process in greater detail. But right now, let's split into groups of four. It's almost spring, so let's see if you can come up with some ideas for routines with a spring-like theme. We'll call it – *New Life*. Off you go!"

Ellie was in a group with Matt, Kate and Justin. The four of them came up with a flower-inspired dance. The lesson was such fun that the time flew by and it wasn't long before Ms Denton was thanking them for their hard work and dismissing them all. Grace, Naomi, Alice, Matt and Nick all stayed behind to find out more about the competition, while Ellie and the others went to shower and get dressed for supper.

That evening in the common room, Ellie and her friends discussed the choreography competition.

"So, you're going to enter are you, Naomi?" asked Lara.

"I'm not sure," Naomi said quietly. She picked at her fingernails, avoiding everybody's gaze.

"Naomi!" Ellie cried at once. "I think you'd be a fab choreographer. You always come up with awesome ideas in our choreo lessons."

"I think you'd be good, too," Lara echoed.

"And it will be really fun! *I'll* dance in your choreography."

"You know, when Ms Denton was telling us about the costumes and music and everything, it did really sound like your sort of thing. You're so creative," Ellie added persuasively.

"And we all know how much you like bossing people around!" Kate joked. "In the nicest possible way, of course!"

A glimmer of a smile appeared on Naomi's face. "Well, when you put it like that, it *does* sound good," she said slowly. "Free reign in the costume room . . . could be fun. And I suppose I've got nothing to lose – except perhaps even more of my pride. . ."

"Oh, pride is overrated anyway," Lara said breezily.

"Pride is a bad thing," Belle said. "How do you say it? It comes before falling down."

The others chuckled. "Kind of," Grace

said. "Pride comes before a fall, we say."

Belle shrugged. "It is the same, I think," she declared. "Anyway, you know what Ms Wells says when anybody falls down in a ballet class: you must jump up straight away and start dancing again!"

Naomi gave her a wink. "You're right, Belle," she said, nodding her head thoughtfully. "I've never been the kind of girl who just slinks off quietly into the sunset, after all."

Lara snorted. "Hardly," she laughed.

Naomi was looking a lot more cheerful. "You guys are right," she announced. "If I've got to go, I'm gonna go out in a blaze of glory. Just think of all the show-stopping numbers I could come up with! I *will* enter the choreo competition!"

"Attagirl!" Ellie cheered. "That sounds more like the Naomi Crawford we know and love."

"Good for you, Naomi," Bryony added.

"And you, Grace? You are going to direct a piece, too?" Belle asked.

Grace nodded. "And Alice," she said. "I think she's already planning in the dorm."

Naomi's eyebrows shot up. "Of course!" she said, nudging Grace. "Grace, we'll have to start picking our dancers quick, before Alice nabs them all."

Grace nodded. "I was thinking that I'd like—"

But Naomi hadn't finished yet. "Ellie, Lara, Bryony, Kate, Belle – you're all going to be needed for my dance," she said in a jokily grand voice. "Who else?"

"Well, surely you need your best buddy Oliver Stafford?" Lara suggested with a mischievous glint in her green eyes.

Naomi grinned. "I was just about to say, not in a million years. But actually, it might be fun to flatter him into agreeing, and then have him dance a really boring role – like an old man!"

"Or something that doesn't even get to move – like a tree!" Bryony suggested.

"He could be a chair that the other dancers get to sit on," Belle offered, grinning at the thought.

Ellie giggled and turned to Grace. "Can you imagine?" she said. "He'd be so mad!" Grace forced a smile in return, and Ellie frowned. "Are you OK?" she asked in a low voice.

Grace blushed. "It's just that ... I don't think it's fair to assume everybody's going to dance in Naomi's piece," she admitted. Then, she spoke loud enough for everyone to hear. "I was hoping some of you would dance in *my* piece." She looked straight at Ellie as she said it.

Naomi blinked, opened her mouth and then closed it. There was a rather awkward silence.

Ellie could see that Grace had a point but, having just bolstered Naomi's confidence, she could also tell that nobody wanted to undermine that by switching allegiance to Grace.

Wanting to lighten the mood, Ellie held up her hands. "Whoa, whoa, no fighting over me, girls," she joked. "I'm sure we can work something out."

"Well, it depends on what kind of dancing you're each going to do," Kate began diplomatically.

Then, Lara joined in. "Who's going to make us the better offer?" she teased, nudging Ellie. "Naomi, Grace, whichever one of you volunteers to make my bed every morning and . . . let's see . . . and do my science homework for me, I'm yours!"

Picking up on what they were doing, Naomi then made a funny face. "Go on, then, Grace," she sighed, pretending to be sorrowful. "*You* can have Oliver. It's a sacrifice I'm willing to make for the sake of our friendship."

But Grace still wasn't smiling. She seemed

seriously upset. And Ellie couldn't see a way of resolving the difficult situation.

Dear Diary,

Help! I feel really torn now. Both Naomi and Grace have made it clear that they want me to dance in their choreo competition pieces, and I don't want to say no to either of them. I mean, my days with Naomi are limited now so I want to spend lots of time with her, and being part of her routine is bound to be great fun. But I've been friends with Grace for longer, plus I know what a big deal this competition is to her — and to her mum, no doubt. What am I going to do? I hope no one else wants me to be in their piece!!

Naomi still seems very up and down. She was really cheerful in the common room this evening, talking about the competition and being really positive about "going out in a blaze of glory". But since we've come back to the dorm, she's just lain on her bed, staring up at the ceiling, looking thoroughly miserable, and not really wanting to speak to anybody. I guess we can't expect her to just snap out of feeling sad about leaving school. Poor Naomi!

Chapter Four

Over the weekend, the choreographers started work in earnest. Naomi had decided on a glamorous Hollywood theme and her piece sounded fairly ambitious from what Ellie could gather, with a large cast of dancers and a rousing soundtrack.

"And of course, I'll be dancing in it, too," she told Ellie, "so naturally, I get the best costume and a solo spot, thank you very much! Director's perks and all that!"

On Saturday afternoon, Grace asked Ellie to help her walk through some ideas for her piece in one of the practice studios. Already, it was obvious to Ellie that Grace and Naomi had completely different approaches. While

Naomi was going for a showy, all-action number, Grace was thinking rather more classically. She had decided to base her routine around an underwater theme, with fewer dancers and a slower, more thoughtful feel.

"I haven't quite chosen my music yet," she confessed to Ellie, "but it's going to be something quite slow-moving and gentle, if you know what I mean. And I was thinking of having just three dancers," she went on, "moving in triangular formations, but constantly flowing and shifting, like the sea."

"Nice," Ellie said approvingly. She couldn't help feeling impressed by how much Grace had thought about this already. Her mind must have been working non-stop ever since Ms Denton announced the competition dates.

"And green and blue costumes, maybe with some spangly bits, like mermaids' tails," Grace went on, "and a dreamy sort of feeling throughout, you know, like when you're swimming underwater and you feel as if you're in another world. What do you think of *Mermaid's Dream* for a title?"

"I think it sounds *wonderful*," Ellie said. "Oh, Grace, I think your ideas sound really fantastic."

"Then be in my choreography!" said Grace, only half-joking.

Ellie sighed. "I'd love to, Grace," she replied honestly. "I really would; it's just. . ."

"I know," said Grace, sighing. "Nobody wants to upset Naomi right now. Neither do I."

"I feel so torn," Ellie said anxiously. "Naomi's only got a few months left here with us, and I want to spend lots of time with her and. . ."

Grace didn't respond.

Ellie felt even worse now. "Of course, I want to spend time with *you*, too, Grace, but. . ." She wrung her hands. "What can I do? There's only one of me!"

Grace smiled wanly. "Wouldn't it be perfect if you had a twin? That would solve everything."

Ellie laughed and gave her friend a hug. "I promise I'll make my mind up soon."

Ellie bumped into Matt as she was leaving the practice studio. "Hello," he said. "I'm looking for an empty studio. Is this one free now?"

Ellie shook her head. "Grace is still in there, working out the first part of her choreo piece," she said.

"Ahh," replied Matt. "I'd better not look in, then. She'll think I'm spying on the competition." He leaned forward conspiratorially. "But you can tell me, Ellie. What's she doing? Any secrets you can tell your old pal, Matt?"

Ellie laughed and pushed him away. "Not likely," she said. "Grace would never forgive me. How's your piece coming along, anyway? Don't tell me – it's a soccer routine where Captain Matt scores the winning goal and does a solo glory dance!"

Matt grinned. "How many times, Ms Brown – it's *football*, not soccer!" he said. "And no, you're wrong there. No footie action in my piece, although I do quite like the Captain Matt thing, now that I think about it." He elbowed her in a friendly way. "So, are you the star of Grace's piece then, or what?"

Ellie gave another big sigh. "Don't ask!" she replied.

Matt raised his eyebrows.

"Grace *does* want me to be in her piece, but Naomi's asked me to be in hers, too," Ellie explained. "And I just can't decide who to choose."

Matt looked awkward. "Right. . ." he said. "I was just about to ask you to be in my piece, too, actually. . ."

"Oh, no! You weren't, were you?" Ellie groaned.

Matt burst out laughing. "Well, luckily for you, Miss Gratitude, I *wasn't*. I was only joking. Otherwise I'd be very offended at that unenthusiastic response!"

Ellie laughed, too. "Sorry, Matt. No offence meant."

"None taken," he said easily. "Mine's an all-boy routine anyway, thanks very much. I wouldn't dream of asking you to dance in it."

"Good," Ellie said happily. "Then I'll leave you to it. See you later."

She smiled as she went back to the dorm to get changed. Matt was such a nice guy. But boy, she was so glad that he really didn't want her in his competition piece. It was bad enough trying to choose between two friends, let alone three!

❄   ❄   ❄

Sunday morning dawned bright and sunny.

"It truly feels like spring today," Ellie said happily, pulling back the dorm curtains. "Look! There's a daffodil out down there!"

"Is everyone coming on the trip today?" Lara asked, sitting up in bed and shaking her hair out of her eyes.

It seemed so. The Royal Ballet School often had trips for students at the weekend. They sometimes went shopping in the nearby high street of East Sheen, or they went to the cinema, or sometimes even into London's West End to see a show.

Today, they were going to the small town of Richmond, just a few minutes' drive away. It sounded like an ideal day out. Richmond had lots of cool shops and pavement cafés, plus some beautiful old buildings and cobbled lanes to wander through. Best of all was the riverside area. The River Thames flowed through Richmond, flanked in the central parts by trendy cafés and terraces and, on the outskirts, by meadows and trees. Ellie just knew it was going to be the perfect place to hang out on hot summer weekends.

It was too cold to spend the afternoon sitting outside just yet though, so, after some serious retail therapy, Ellie and her friends settled down in a cheerful little café in the cobbled lanes and treated themselves to mugs of hot chocolate and little sweet tarts called Maids of Honour. Ellie was delighted to learn that the recipe for the tarts was invented hundreds of years ago in one of the royal palaces and kept secret until Henry VIII discovered it and made the tarts famous.

"This is the life," Ellie said happily, unwinding her scarf.

"Isn't it just," murmured Naomi, sipping her hot chocolate. "If only things could stay like this," she added quietly.

Ellie reached over and squeezed her arm.

"Oh, sorry, Naomi, I wasn't thinking," she said hurriedly. She could have kicked herself.

Naomi bit into her Maid of Honour. "It's all right, Ell," she assured her. "You don't have to stop feeling happy about being here just because I'm going."

Lara gazed at Naomi over the rim of her mug. "Have you thought any further about what you're going to do, Naomi?" she asked.

Naomi shook her head. "Not yet," she said. "But there's loads of time to think about that." She shrugged. "I mean, Ms Bell was really supportive and nice when I saw her on Wednesday, and my parents always ask about it when they call, but it all seems like too big a decision to have to make right now. The only decision I feel capable of making at the moment is whether or not to have another tart."

"And will you?" asked Kate.

Naomi pretended to think about it deeply.

"Well, after careful analysis of all the facts — deliciousness of these tarts, money left in purse, reputation to consider as greedy pig — and serious weighing up of all the pros and cons, I'm going to say ... yes, of course I'm going to have another one!" She got to her feet. "Anybody else want anything while I'm up there?"

As Naomi went up to the counter, Lara raised her eyebrows. "I guess that means she doesn't want to talk about it," she said dryly.

"I guess not," Ellie agreed.

Dear Diary,

Wondering what Naomi's going to choose to do instead of ballet has made me think more about my own future. I still would love nothing more than to be a ballerina, obviously, but then Naomi and Kelly said that too, and look what's happened to them! There's no guarantee I'll get my wish either.

I can't help wondering what we'll all be doing in ten years' time. Will any of us have made it into The Royal Ballet?

Chapter Five

Sunday night was decision night. Grace and Naomi had been working hard on their presentation documents. After the two choreographers had run through their ideas with their friends, it was time for the dancers to decide who they would dance for. They agreed that they would all do it as a group to keep it straightforward.

Belle began. "Naomi, Grace, I think both of your pieces sound *formidable* – fantastic!" she said. "But I am choosing to accept Grace's invitation. I am more comfortable with the more classical style. And also. . ." She gave a dainty shrug. "I have always wanted to be a mermaid!"

The girls all laughed.

"Me, too," said Bryony. "I hope you don't mind, Naomi."

"Not at all," Naomi said easily, as Grace hugged Belle and Bryony. "Lara, what about you?"

"Belle's right, it is a horrible decision to make, but I'm going with you, Naomi," Lara said. "I hope you don't mind, Grace. Your piece sounds wonderful, but I've always been a sucker for Hollywood drama."

"Fabulous!" Naomi cried, giving Lara a high-five.

It was Kate's turn next. "Well, the piece that appeals most to me is Naomi's," she said slowly, looking really uncomfortable at having to choose. "I've always had a thing about old films." She glanced uncertainly at Grace.

Grace leaned over and patted Kate's arm. "I know it's nothing personal."

Kate smiled, with a look of sheer relief.

"I'm glad you understand,'" she said.

And then Grace turned to Ellie. "You're the last one to choose," she said. "What are you going to do?"

Ellie took a deep breath, and made a decision. "If it's OK with you guys, I'm going to say yes to both of you," she said. "I've tried and tried to make a choice between you, but I just can't. You are both my friends, and both of your pieces sound really cool. I know it will be hard, and I hope you're both OK with it. But this is the only way I know to do the right thing."

"Are you sure?" Grace asked. "It's going to mean a lot of extra work, you know, Ellie."

"I know that," said Ellie, "but there's just no other way around it. I can't choose between you two, and that's all there is to it."

"Well, that's great news," Naomi said, coming over to hug her. "Don't worry, I'll make sure you have some really fantastic bits to dance, Ellie."

"Brilliant," Grace said happily. "Ellie, Belle and Bryony – that's my three!"

"Who else is going to be in your group, Naomi?" Ellie asked curiously. "I can see a lot of names on your list there."

Naomi counted up her dancers. "I'm going to have six girls and four boys," she said. "Me, you, Kate, Lara, Megan and Holly, plus Justin, Simon, Toby and Joe, I hope."

Ellie whistled. "Phew! You're going to have your work cut out for you," she said.

Naomi laughed. "Do you reckon? I was actually feeling rather pleased about how many people I'll have to boss about!"

Year 7 choreographers Grace, Naomi, Alice, Matt and Nick all handed in their names and cast lists to Ms Denton the following day after lunch.

"I'm so excited," Grace said, her eyes shining, as she and Ellie walked to their geography lesson. "I've booked a practice studio for a couple of nights this week. I thought we could start running through the routine. There's only two weeks before the pre-selection process!"

"Sure," said Ellie. "Just let me know where and when, and I'll be there."

During the geography lesson, Ellie noticed that everybody seemed very distracted. Matt was whispering to the boys nearest to him, and Alice was deep in conversation with Scarlett and Rebecca.

Their teacher, Mr Whitehouse, had noticed too. "Naomi Crawford, is that a note I just saw you passing?" he said with a frown.

Naomi was all wide-eyed innocence. "Who, sir? Me, sir?"

"Yes, Naomi. You, Naomi," said Mr Whitehouse. "Come up here please, and bring that note you were trying to pass to Lara McCloud."

Naomi's face fell as she trudged up to the front of the classroom and guiltily handed over the crumpled bit of paper.

"First meeting tonight, six-fifteen, Ashton Studio," Mr Whitehouse read aloud. "I'm not *quite* sure what this has to do with mapping, Ms Crawford," he said sternly. "It sounds more like a rehearsal schedule to me."

"Ahh . . . well, you see . . . I was just about to add a map to my note, sir," said Naomi, improvising quickly. "I wanted to experience what you were teaching us in . . . um . . . in a *practical* way, by practising my map-drawing skills in relation to what you were saying!" She beamed up at him brightly.

Mr Whitehouse's lips twitched. "Well, you're certainly very *practical* when it comes to making up good excuses, Naomi," he said.

Naomi blinked. "Excuses, sir? I'm not sure

what you mean, sir," she replied innocently.

Ellie could tell their teacher was trying his hardest not to smile at Naomi's fabrication. She was finding it pretty tricky not to laugh herself.

"You know, if you aren't lucky enough to end up a geography teacher like me, you'll be an extremely good actress, Naomi," said Mr Whitehouse. "I'll tell you what. As you're so keen to get some practical experience drawing maps, you can stay up here with me and help me draw the next map on the blackboard."

The whole class burst out laughing at the horrified look on Naomi's face.

Naomi grinned and held up her hands. "It's a fair cop, sir," she said, good-naturedly. "Now, which map are we drawing first?"

At tuck that afternoon, Naomi pulled out her diary. "Attention all dancers in my group," she said in an official-sounding voice. "As Mr

Whitehouse kindly announced for me in geography, rehearsals start tonight at six-fifteen in the Ashton Studio, followed by the same time Wednesday and Friday."

"Blimey! Do we only get Tuesday and Thursday nights off?" Lara asked, pretending to wipe sweat from her brow.

Naomi grinned. "My favourite soap is on Tuesday and Thursday nights," she said.

"Hold on a minute, Naomi," Grace piped up anxiously. "Your rehearsals clash with mine. I've booked the Pavlova Studio for tonight and Wednesday, six-fifteen to seven-fifteen."

"No worries, I've booked the Ashton," Naomi said, chomping into a muesli bar. She grinned. "We were so lucky to get studio time, you know. Students end up practising all over the place for the competition – in the changing rooms, in dorms, in the courtyard, even!"

"Um . . . guys," Ellie said. "I can't be in two places at once. And if you're both doing rehearsals tonight and Wednesday. . ."

Grace and Naomi both looked at her. "Ahh. . ." they said in unison.

"Yes," said Ellie, feeling wretched. She wanted to dance well for both her friends. But how was she going to manage that, if she was going to miss out on some of the rehearsals?

Grace looked at Naomi. "Well, you've got Ellie to yourself on Friday," she said, "so maybe I could have her on Wednesday night."

"And tonight?" Naomi asked.

"We'll have to share her," Grace decided. "Half an hour each. Or—"

"Guys!" Ellie cried. "I am right here, at the table! Don't I get a say in this?"

Grace and Naomi both looked guiltily at her. "Sorry," they said in unison.

"Well, maybe you could go to Grace between six-fifteen and six-forty-five, then come to me between six-forty-five and seven-fifteen," Naomi suggested. She grinned. "Let's face it, it'll probably take me half an hour to get started, won't it?"

"Grace, is that OK with you?" Ellie asked.

Grace gave a satisfied nod. "That would make it half and half."

Ellie sighed, scribbling the times down in her diary. "Let's do that, then," she said. "I can see this is going to be a complicated week!" She stuffed her diary back in her bag. "Come on, we'd better run," she said, glancing at the clock on the wall. "Choreo class is in five minutes, and I'm sure neither of you hot-shot choreographers want to miss *that*."

Naomi made an annoyed clicking noise with her tongue. "Will you tell Ms Denton I'm going to be late?" she asked the others. "I've got another meeting with Ms Bell now." She frowned. "Typical. Why can't I get to miss something like physics or maths, instead of it clashing with the class I really *do* want to go to!"

"Sure, I'll tell Ms Denton," Ellie agreed, getting to her feet. "Good luck!"

Naomi grimaced. "I'll need it," she said gloomily. "My parents are going to be coming down for the next careers session, so I'm going to have to start thinking about what I want to do – and fast!"

Once again, Naomi didn't give much away about her careers session as the girls all sat down for supper. She changed the subject when they asked about it, saying she was too busy thinking about her first choreo practice. *Which is fair enough*, Ellie thought to herself. None of them could think about much else right now!

For all her misgivings about signing up for two choreo pieces, Ellie still felt a buzz of excitement as she, Grace, Belle and Bryony went along to the Pavlova Studio that evening for their first rehearsal. She'd heard a couple of Grace's ideas and walked through some of the movements with her, but she knew that her friend had been busily thinking out her routine since then and was sure to have developed it a good deal further.

Grace's cheeks were flushed as she and her dancers sat cross-legged in the middle of the studio and she explained her piece. "As you know, I've come up with a piece called *Mermaid's Dream*," she told them. "I want it to be flowing and dreamy. I want to try and capture that feeling of swimming underwater in the sea, your hair streaming behind you, that deep calm and serenity, if you know what I mean?"

Ellie nodded.

"Sounds lovely," Bryony commented.

Grace got to her feet. "Let me show you the starting position," she said, "then I'll play you the music I've chosen."

Ellie, Bryony and Belle let themselves be

arranged into a triangular formation, all facing the centre. Grace positioned them so that they had one leg stretching back behind the other, and their arms reaching up into the air, palms together, fingers pointing up. "Eyes closed, please," Grace added, "and I'll play you the music."

The piece of music began with the sound of waves crashing on to a pebbly beach, before moving into a gentle flowing harmony of piano and flute. Ellie's whole body began to relax at the calming music. "This is gorgeous, Grace," she murmured.

"It makes me feel as if I am in a dream already," Belle added.

When the music had come to an end Grace switched off the tape, looking pleased. "Good, that's just what I hoped you'd say," she said. "Now, this is what I'd like you to do. . ."

Ellie became so engrossed in Grace's ideas and movements for her piece, she couldn't believe it when the alarm on her watch reminded her that it was six-forty-five already. Time to go to her second rehearsal of the evening! "Sorry, guys, I've got to go to the rival camp now," she said. She was enjoying herself so much, it was hard to go.

"No problem," Grace said. "I'll stand in for you. Thanks, Ellie. See you later."

Ellie slipped out of the studio and made her way towards the Ashton Studio. As she approached she could hear laughter and loud music coming all the way along the corridor. A very different sort of rehearsal seemed to be taking place there! She grinned to herself. By the sound of it, there was going to be no calmness and dreaming in *this* group – that much was clear!

"Ellie Brown! Delighted you could join us," Naomi cried, as Ellie entered the studio. "Welcome to Team Crawford."

Ellie waved and said hello to everybody,

gazing around curiously as she pulled off her sweatpants. All the boys appeared to be getting ready to swing imaginary golf clubs, while the girls wove in between them. "I thought you were doing a Hollywood theme?" she called over, feeling puzzled.

"I am. Fifties starlets!" Naomi said. "Think pearls and satin, big hair, fabulous old movie stars!"

"Marilyn Monroe," put in Lara helpfully.

"And . . . golf?" Ellie asked, still feeling none the wiser.

Naomi stared at Ellie and then at the boys. "No!" she giggled. "They're pretending to be leaning on canes!" she explained.

Ellie laughed. "OK, OK, I think I'm getting your look now. Sounds fab."

"Oh, it will be," Naomi assured her. "Utterly fab. Shall I show you what we've got so far?"

"Yes, please," Ellie said.

Naomi had chosen a big band soundtrack, with a jazzy swing-beat that Ellie loved. There was humour in her piece too, with the boys being asked to make eyes at the girls, or swing around on their canes rakishly, in a way that Ellie could see was going to look really funny on stage.

"So, Ellie, if you could come here, between Lara and Kate," Naomi called, "this is where you'll be starting." She ran backwards a few metres to consider the effect, and then pursed her lips. "Actually, scrub that. Ellie, you'd be better on the other side of Lara, next to Holly. Otherwise we've got all the taller ones at one end and... Yes, that's better," she said in satisfaction, as Ellie switched places.

"This has been so much fun, so far," whispered Kate, as Naomi finished positioning everyone.

"It certainly looks it!" Ellie agreed. "What's your piece called, Naomi?" Ellie called out from her position. "Have you decided yet?"

Naomi shook her head. "Not yet. I want it to be something linked to old Hollywood movies – you know, those lovely screwball comedies where everybody's falling in love with everybody else? I need a title that sums all of that up, but still has a dance feeling, if you know what I mean. It needs to have some movement in it."

"*Social Butterflies*," Kate suggested.

Naomi raised her eyebrows. "Not bad," she said thoughtfully.

"*The Wings of Love*," called out Holly.

Naomi shook her head. "Ooh, that's romantic! I'll have a think about that one, too," she decided. "Anyway, let's start from the top. With luck the perfect title is going to come to me in my sleep. Right! Everybody in starting positions? Ellie, we're going to begin with each girl stepping forward between the boys, doing a curtsey, like a kind of introduction, then the boys will step forward, turn, and take one hand of each of the two girls in front of him. So Kate and I, as we're at each end of the line of girls, we get only one hand held, but all the other girls should have both hands taken, by different boys. Sounds complicated but it works, OK?"

Ellie nodded.

"It's like in those old films where people are playing different characters off against each other, that kind of thing," Naomi went on. "Now, ladies, I want each of your curtseys to be as elaborate and over-the-top as you like, yeah? Ready? Here comes the music!"

Dear Diary,

I really enjoyed both my rehearsals tonight, but, boy, you just couldn't imagine two more different styles if you tried! Grace and Naomi have such different ways of working. Grace had thought out almost her entire routine in her head before she started working with her dancers. Naomi, on the other hand, is much more experimental – trying things out, keeping some ideas, discarding others, until she's happy.

But the interesting thing is, both ways seem to work. I think both pieces are going to look fantastic; I really do!

Chapter Six

"Good morning, girls! Rise and shine!"

At the sound of Mrs Hall's voice Ellie forced one bleary eye open, and then the other. Was it really morning again already? She felt as if she'd only just got into bed. Her dreams this week had been exhausting: full of choreo rehearsals that went on and on for hours, and then Phoebe and Bethany, her friends from Oxford, had burst into one of the rehearsals demanding to know why Ellie hadn't replied to their e-mails and letters yet!

Ellie yawned and pulled her pillow over her head. It wasn't that she was regretting her decision to join both choreo groups for the competition, it was more that she felt she had no time to do anything else. Her homework was piling up, as was the list of people she owed e-mails to. She was never going to get on top of it all!

"Are you all right, there, Ellie?" Grace asked from the next bed. "Not going back to sleep, are you?"

Ellie groaned and sat up. It felt like the most enormous effort to keep herself upright. "I wish," she said, pulling on her dressing gown. "I'm going to sleep right through this weekend."

"Oh no, you're not, Ellie Brown," Naomi called down from her bed. "More rehearsals, remember? We've got to be ready for the pre-selection judging next week, haven't we?"

"Sorry, Ell, but I'm going to need you too," Grace said apologetically. "We've got to get that ending right. I think I've worked out how to do it now, but we need to practise a few more times."

"OK, OK," Ellie said good-naturedly, as she grabbed her washbag and headed towards the showers. Maybe a jet of hot water would help her wake up. *Something* was going to have to!

Ellie was just shampooing her hair when she suddenly heard a familiar voice belting out a show-tune in the next cubicle. Ellie raised her eyebrows at the sound, and then a smile slid over her face. Naomi was singing again! That really *was* good news.

It had become a part of dorm life for the Year 7 girls to hear Naomi cheerfully singing in the shower every morning. After her appraisal, though, the singing had stopped. Ellie and the others had missed hearing Naomi's glorious voice hitting the high notes as she washed her hair. The dorm had seemed a quieter, more subdued place without the morning concert. Now, Ellie hoped it was back for good.

✽   ✽   ✽

Ellie certainly wasn't the only one feeling the strain of the extra work. Everyone was tense and tired, worn out from practising for the competition, especially the choreographers themselves. Perfectionist Grace was, as usual, worrying endlessly about tiny details, not sleeping well, talking of nothing else but her piece. Matt was looking tired and pre-occupied, as were Alice and Nick. But Naomi . . . Naomi seemed to be *thriving* on all the pressure, as she rushed around briefing her dancers whenever she came up with a new idea. Her eyes were bright, her smile was back; a long scrawled list of things she had to do seemed to be permanently attached to her hand.

There was still no mention of any decisions she'd made regarding her future, however. And it wasn't until one evening in the dorm that Ellie learned something new. Grace, Bryony and Belle were all showering after their Friday Dalcroze class, and Kate was in the Slip, practising the piano.

Ellie and Naomi were waiting to use the showers, and Ellie was just untying her bun when her hairband shot off with a *ping*! It flew right over Grace's bed and landed on the floor between Grace and Naomi's beds.

"Are you throwing things at me, Ms Brown?" Naomi joked, untying her own bun carefully.

Ellie laughed and went to find her hairband. She crouched down to pick it up, but then something caught her eye under Naomi's bed. "What's this?" she asked curiously, pulling it out. "A magazine?"

She held up the glossy brochure to show Naomi.

Naomi looked away. "Oh, just something Ms Bell gave me," she said. "It's some school or other. I haven't actually looked at it yet."

Ellie studied the cover of the school

brochure with interest. It was a performing arts school. There was a collage of pictures showing pupils performing at a whole range of shows – a theatrical production, a music group playing guitars and singing into microphones on stage, a mime show, a row of costumed can-can girls kicking up their legs together and beaming. . .

"This looks cool," she said, flicking through the pages. "You should check it out. It says here you can study dance, drama, singing, choreography, mime, theatre skills. . ."

Naomi hesitated. "I'm so busy with this competition, Ellie; I just haven't had time," she said, rather lamely. "I *will* look through them all once the shortlist has been decided, though."

"You'll look through them *all*?" Ellie echoed. "Why, how many have you got under there?" She bent down and saw four or five similar brochures in a messy pile. Clearly,

Naomi had just shoved them under there without a second glance. "Naomi!" she cried. "If you're not going to look through these, I will!" she said, threateningly, pulling the other brochures out. "Wow – these look awesome! Honestly! Way better than any regular school would be. We all know it would be a crime for you to go back to one of those."

Naomi came around to Ellie's side of the bed and looked over her shoulder at the fan of brochures Ellie was showing her. "All right, all right. You sound like my parents!" she said, holding up her hands. "I'll look at them tonight, OK?"

Naomi was as good as her word and sat down with her pile of reading after supper. She invited all her friends to look, too.

"Wow, this looks brilliant," marvelled Kate, as she flicked through the pages of one brochure. "As well as the usual classes in drama, dance and music, you can also study costume design, make-up, lighting, stage management, prop design. . ."

"Which is that one?" Naomi asked. She sounded interested, Ellie was pleased to note.

"It's in Manchester – your home town," Kate said, tossing the brochure over to her. "Here, have a look."

Naomi picked it up and started flicking through.

"And *this* school is right in central London," Grace added, reading through a printed sheet.

"We could smuggle you into our dorm every night," Ellie joked. "Rent-free. And you could sneak back every morning!"

"This one in Edinburgh sounds good too!" Belle said, leafing through another brochure. "Oh, these pictures! What a beautiful place to live!"

"Yeah, but it's miles from *us*," Bryony pointed out. "We'd never see you again."

Naomi looked up from the Manchester brochure. "Of course you would," she scoffed. "I'll be on telly every night in a soap opera, or costume dramas. I've always fancied myself in one of those corsets. Or I might star in a touring production of *Annie*. Tell you what, I'll make sure you lot all have front row tickets, my treat!"

Ellie laughed. She was so pleased that she'd accidentally found Naomi's stash of school brochures! At last, Naomi was starting to sound really positive about life beyond The Royal Ballet School.

"*Annie?*" Lara was protesting. "I'll have you know, if any red-heads are required, there's one right here who doesn't need a wig!"

"All right, *Grease*, then," Naomi replied, sticking out her tongue. "Hey, I'll even be one of the girls in *The Sound of Music* if it gets me on a stage."

"Do-re-mi-fa-so-la-te-do!" Ellie trilled, managing to miss every single note.

Naomi put her hands over her ears. "Ouch!" she yelped. "I said *The Sound of Music*, Ell, not The Sound of Torture!"

Ellie laughed and whacked Naomi over the head with one of her brochures. "Just for that, I *will* be in the front row of your first show — and I'll sing along with all your words to distract you," she threatened. "That'll teach you to trash my singing, Naomi Crawford!"

"Ooh," Naomi said, with a shudder. "Don't, Ellie. That really is the stuff of nightmares."

Dear Diary,

Finally I've grabbed some time to write! It's good to see Naomi thinking about her future. I can totally see her on stage in Annie or Grease. And it's really good to see her excited again.

All this talk about careers and futures does make me wonder what I would do without life at The Royal Ballet School. Ballet is the *only thing I can imagine doing; it's the only thing I want to do! I'm certainly not cut out for singing and dancing at a performance art school, not with <u>my</u> singing!*

I'm just going to have to hope that I make it through all my appraisals and auditions, and stay at The Royal Ballet School until I've become a professional ballerina.

The next week felt like a blur of non-stop rehearsals to Ellie. Life at The Royal Ballet School had always been busy, but now Ellie felt as if she was on a treadmill that was going faster and faster. Any minute now she was going to fall off and land in a heap of un-finished homework, unanswered letters, and her unwritten diary.

Finally, it was the day of the choreography competition pre-selection. It took the place of their usual Wednesday afternoon choreo lesson.

Alice's team was first to present their piece to Ms Bell, the Lower School Ballet Principal. Alice had called her piece *Honeybee*, and she, Scarlett and Rebecca all wore cute little bee antennae as they zipped through their routine to a jaunty piece of music.

Ellie watched critically, trying to see how it measured up to both Grace's and Naomi's pieces. It was hard not to be biased, but she didn't think Alice's routine flowed quite as well as Grace's or had the originality and pizazz that Naomi's had.

Then it was Grace's turn. "Don't forget to smile," she told Ellie, Belle and Bryony anxiously, though she looked as if she might forget herself. "And remember it's *two* pirouettes at the end now, not three. You need to start them as soon as you hear the waves again at the end of the music."

"Don't worry, Grace," Belle said. "We will be true mermaids for you."

Grace hugged them all. "I know you will. Good luck," she said.

Ellie felt her heart beat a little faster as she and the others got into position and Grace started the tape. Ellie shut her eyes, listening to the familiar sound of waves that opened the track, waiting for her cue and . . . away they went.

The routine opened with a *port de bras* sequence with the three of them deliberately dancing out of sync to create a flowing, wave-like mood. "As long as nobody thinks it's a Mexican wave," Grace had said anxiously the first time they had practised it.

Ellie remembered the comment now and found it hard to believe that Grace had ever doubted the calm opening sequence could be misinterpreted. She, Belle and Bryony had worked hard to make sure that as Ellie began her movement by bending forward to the ground, Belle was halfway through hers, twisting sideways, and Bryony's back and arms were arched gracefully back. "Let your arms feel as loose and flexible as if they were being swirled around by an ocean wave," Grace had instructed them. "Your feet, meanwhile, are firmly rooted into the ocean floor!"

After the *port de bras* sequence, the three of them *chasséd* into an *arabesque*, stretching their raised leg to ninety degrees, facing one another in the centre of their triangle. Then they waltzed to the side and *chasséd* into a second *arabesque*.

Ellie felt light as air as she travelled through the steps. Grace had coached them all so thoroughly that each girl knew exactly what she should be doing. Before Ellie knew it, the music was fading and it was time for their double *pirouette*, before assuming the closing position as the sound of the waves faded back in to signify the end. They'd done it! And they'd done it well. One look at Grace's pleased face spoke volumes.

Matt's piece, *The Soldier*, came next. The boys marching on to the stage strong and slow gave Matt's piece a sinister feel and as the four boys saluted, it was clear that this was going to be a dramatic piece of theatre.

Then, it was Nick's piece, *A Clown Convention*. Nick had always had a thing about clowns and he had managed to persuade Kirsty and Neil to dress in baggy striped pyjama style costumes and wear big red noses. Their deliberately wobbly *arabesques* and muddled *allegro* steps made them look just like clowns!

Finally, it was time for Naomi's team. "Enjoy yourselves, guys," she told them. "Think glamour! Think showbiz! Let's dazzle 'em!"

Ellie felt far more relaxed about dancing Naomi's piece than she had about Grace's. Naomi seemed to never get flustered or nervous when it came to performing, and perhaps her being more relaxed rubbed off on her group.

Naomi handed in her presentation documents to Ms Bell and did a neat curtsey. "This is called *Social Butterflies*," she said. "But I'm afraid that's only a working title. I haven't quite settled on a final title yet."

Ms Bell nodded. "Thank you, Naomi," she said.

The music for Naomi's piece began, and Ellie was off again. Even without the glamorous Hollywood costumes, wigs and make-up that Naomi had planned for the team if they made it through to the final round, the routine was really fun.

Ellie caught a glimpse of the Ballet Principal smiling, appreciating the comedy that Naomi had woven in as she and the other girls did a series of *pas de chats* away from the boys with their hands up in alarm when the boys had pretended to try and kiss them. The boys then pursued the girls around the stage until the pitch of the music changed, which was the girls' cue to have a change of heart and start pursuing the boys instead, all the way off-stage.

Ms Bell was chuckling, Ellie noticed with glee.

"Thank you," Ms Bell said. "And thank you everybody else. You may now leave the room, and send in the Year 8s please."

So that was it. Ellie and her friends had to wait until the Ballet Principal had properly evaluated all of the entries before they'd know which, if any, of their pieces were good enough to be entered into the competition.

"We did really well, I think," Naomi said as they went back towards their dorm to get changed for supper. "Good work, everybody." She turned back to Grace. "And your piece — wow, Grace, it was so beautiful! I could never have done something like that in a million years. Sheer class, that's what you are, girl!"

Grace laughed and tucked an arm into Naomi's. "You know what? I thought yours was great, too. And I thought exactly the same thing – that I'd never have the nerve to try something so big and theatrical as you did."

"Aw shucks," Naomi said, trying and failing to sound modest. "Let's face it, Grace. We both rocked!"

Ellie smiled to herself as they went into the dorm. It was nice to hear both Naomi and Grace sounding so pleased after all the work they'd put in lately. She really hoped they'd both be as happy the next morning, when the results were announced.

Dear Diary,
It's a waiting game now, until we find out whose pieces have made it through to the competition. I feel confident that both

Grace and Naomi's routines were good enough — but then ALL of the pieces from our year were pretty good. And who knows how amazing the Year 8 pieces were? We'll just have to hope it's good news.

On Thursday morning, as Ellie and her friends were having breakfast, Ms Denton came into the dining room with a list in her hand. "I was just about to pin this on the noticeboard, but thought I'd tell you in person, too, who's going through to the next round of the competition," she said.

Everybody put down their cutlery to listen, and Naomi grabbed Grace's hand across the table. "Good luck," she said quickly.

Ms Denton pulled up an extra chair and sat down at the table. "The judges thought all five of the Year 7 pieces were extremely good," she began. "All of them struck us as fresh, original and carefully put together, with good use of space and musicality. We could see how much work you all put into this competition. So well done, all of you, choreographers and dancers alike." She smiled around the table, and then cleared her throat. "After much discussion, we have decided to put three of the pieces through: Grace, Nick and Naomi, congratulations, you're all going through to the next round. Alice and Matt, I'm very sorry, but you didn't quite make it this time. You were both near misses, if that's any consolation. I do hope you'll try again next year."

Ellie glanced down the table to where Matt was sitting, looking crestfallen. Alice sat with her head bowed, being comforted by Scarlett. But Naomi and Grace were whooping and cheering, as was Nick.

"Well done, Team Crawford!" Naomi cried, sending her cereal spoon flying in the excitement. "Fantastic!"

Grace hugged Ellie, then Bryony and Belle.

"Thank you, thank you," she said to them. "This means so much to me!"

After breakfast, as they put on their ballet things in the dorm for their morning class, Grace quickly phoned her mum to tell her the news. "I got through! I'm in the choreo competition!" she cried into her mobile, joy and relief all over her face. Ellie could see from Grace's smile that her mum must be just as happy on the other end of the phone.

Naomi, too, was making a jubilant phonecall home. Afterwards, she lay on her bed for a few seconds, smiling broadly.

"I am so glad for you, Naomi," Ellie told her. "You deserve this. You worked really hard."

"I did, didn't I?" Naomi said, scrambling up and pulling on her leotard. "You know, I hadn't quite realized how much it mattered to me until now. If I'd failed. . ." She shuddered, not finishing her sentence. "I don't know if I could have coped with another knockback, you know. But getting a bit of acclaim for a change feels *soooo* good!" She wriggled her arms into her leotard and looked over at Grace, who'd just finished her call. "Hey, I think we ought to celebrate, don't you, Grace? How about a midnight feast on Friday night?"

Grace glanced down the dorm in Alice's direction. "Don't you think it might be a bit . . . insensitive?" she asked. "I mean, not everybody got through, did they? Alice might not feel like celebrating."

Naomi frowned. "You're right," she said. She was just about to go over to Alice, when Alice came rushing up to her instead.

"Naomi, Grace, well done!" she said generously. "I thought your pieces were both really fab."

"Oh, thanks, Alice," Grace said. "And I'm really sorry yours didn't get through too."

"Me, too," Naomi said. "I loved your antennae – so cute!" Then she hesitated.

"Alice, we were talking about having a dorm party tomorrow at midnight, after Mrs Hall goes to sleep. But we'll understand if you don't feel like it right now. What do you think?"

Alice smiled. "I think it sounds a great idea," she said. "It's just what I need to cheer me up."

Naomi grinned. "I was hoping you'd say that," she said. "So we're on for tomorrow night, yeah? Everybody try and smuggle as much stuff up to the dorm from your tuck boxes as is humanly possible, OK?"

"OK, boss!" Lara laughed.

"Oh, and guys in my team," Naomi said, "you've all got the night off tonight. Don't ever let it be said that I'm a slave driver!"

The thought of a midnight feast and dorm party kept the Year 7 girls buoyed up and in giggly moods all the way through Thursday and Friday.

"What is it with you girls?" Matt asked

rather impatiently, as they whispered and giggled their way through Friday afternoon's history and science lessons.

"Nothing that boys need to know about," Lara teased. "What's up, Matt? Feeling left out?"

Ellie was surprised to see an uncharacteristic scowl cross Matt's face.

"Oh, leave me alone," he snapped, turning his back.

Kate raised her eyebrows at Lara. "Who's rattled his cage?" she asked.

Ellie guessed Matt was still feeling bad about not having made it through to the choreography competition. She knew he'd worked very hard on his piece and had had high hopes of performing in front of the judges.

Poor Matt. Ellie was beginning to realize that a dancer had to be tough mentally as well as physically to cope with the inevitable setbacks that came as part of a dancer's life. She knew that she'd almost certainly have her own setbacks too.

Dear Diary,

We're all in bed, waiting for Mrs Hall to come and switch the lights out. Naomi, Belle and Kate have all set their alarm clocks on low, but I bet nobody's feeling very sleepy with the thought of the party later on. We've all managed to sneak some goodies into the dorm. Naomi even wrapped up a slice of apple pie in a napkin after supper tonight and has hidden it under her bed!

I don't think I'll manage to pretend to be going to sleep. I feel much too giggly and excited! But I'll sign off now, as Mrs Hall should be in any minute!

Chapter Seven

"Wake up! Wake up! It's midnight!"

Ellie had been dreaming about mermaids when Naomi shook her awake. "What? Who's that?" she murmured, but then, seconds later, her eyes popped open and she remembered. The midnight feast! The dorm party!

She grabbed her dressing gown and torch and went to join the rest of the girls in the centre of the room, where everybody was laying out the food and drink they'd sneaked upstairs.

Ellie ripped open a bag of crisps she'd smuggled from her tuck box, and grabbed a handful. Somehow, knowing that the food and drink was strictly forbidden made it all the tastier!

"I wonder if every class does this their first year," Kate said quietly.

Belle said, "Maybe next year's girls will be more obedient than we are!"

"Can you believe that next year, there will be a whole new crop of Year 7s that we'll have to show around?" Ellie whispered.

Naomi looked a little sad. "I'll have to leave an instruction manual on how to get seconds from the lunch lady and how to swipe cake from the dining room."

"Definitely," Ellie said gently.

"Anybody know any ghost stories?" Lara whispered, changing the subject and shining her torch under her chin so that it lit up her face with a spooky yellow glow.

"I can tell you about the ghost I once saw," Naomi said, shining her own flashlight under her chin.

"You saw a ghost?" Belle cried. Her hand, still holding a half-eaten cookie, paused on its way up to her mouth. "Really?"

Naomi nodded. "Really," she said.

Bryony shuddered. "What happened?"

Naomi's face was grave. "Are you sure you want to hear this?" she asked solemnly, sipping her cup of juice. "It's kind of scary."

"Are you kidding? Of course we do," Lara said. "Even more so now. Tell us about your ghost at once!"

Naomi nodded. "OK, but don't say I didn't warn you," she said. She put her cup down, cleared her throat, and spoke in a quiet voice. "Here's what happened. I was staying in my aunt's cottage one night, and she lives right in the middle of the Yorkshire Moors. There's just the one little cottage on this dark, dark road, surrounded by fields and forest. It's kind of a creepy place even when it's day." She paused for breath. "And I woke up in the middle of the night with this weird feeling that someone – or something – was in the house that shouldn't be."

"Oh, no," groaned Grace with a shiver. "I'm not sure I want to hear this!"

"Sssshhh," Naomi warned. "Not so loud. So I was peering around in the darkness, trying to see if anything was there, when I heard this creepy kind of howling noise, very, very faint, like this: *A-whooo-whooo. A-whoo-whooo*."

"The wind in the trees outside," Ellie guessed. "The night train going by."

"No," said Naomi in hushed tones. "There was no wind. There was no train. It was a sound I'd never heard before. I lay there in bed, with the covers pulled right up to my chin, my heart was pounding away in fright. Then I started to feel really, really cold. My toes felt like little icicles. And my nose was like an ice cube. And there were goosebumps creeping up all over my skin."

The room was silent. Nobody was eating or

drinking any more; they had all stopped to listen to Naomi's spooky story.

"Then I heard footsteps," Naomi said. "Slow, dragging footsteps outside my door getting nearer . . . and nearer . . . and nearer. . ."

Ellie held her breath and hugged her knees tight to her.

"The door creaked open," Naomi went on. "I hardly dared to watch it. And I was getting colder and colder under my aunt's blanket. I was absolutely freezing! And then, as I watched, this . . . this woman came in, all in white, with the whitest face you've ever seen. I could hardly see her, she was so pale, dressed in a long white nightgown with this candlestick in her hand. And it was as if she was *flickering* as she moved. When she stepped in front of the door, I could see straight through her."

"I don't like this story any more," Grace

whimpered, shuffling up close to Ellie.

"She came further into the room," Naomi went on, dropping her voice even lower. "And then slowly, slowly she turned and stared right at me. Her eyes were like these terrible dark pools of misery. I just knew there and then that something awful had happened to her."

"Oh, no," Kate moaned. "I don't want to know."

"She reached out towards me," Naomi said, "stretching out this bony white hand, and I was just frozen to the spot. I tried to shout out to my parents but I couldn't even move my mouth."

There was a pause. "Go on," Lara urged. "What happened next?"

"She came closer to me and leaned over to my face," Naomi went on. "I could *smell* her and everything. She smelled of death and mould and bad things. And she came closer and closer, right up to my ear, and then she opened her mouth so close that I could feel her breath on my face, and she was leaning right over me, almost touching me, and she said . . . BOO!"

Every girl in the room jumped and screamed at Naomi's shout, and Naomi collapsed into giggles.

"Naomi!" yelled Lara, the first to recover. "That was soooo mean!"

"What did she really say? I don't understand," Belle wailed.

Naomi was helpless with giggles. "She didn't say anything, silly," she spluttered. "I made the whole thing up."

Everyone was laughing now, relieved that the story was over. "Naomi Crawford, I'm never going to believe another word you say," Ellie protested. "Of all the low-down dirty tricks!"

"Sorry, guys," Naomi chuckled. "You should have seen your faces, though!"

The door swung open just then, and made them all jump again.

"The ghost!" squealed Grace, clutching Ellie again.

"No, not the ghost," came a grim voice. "The very cross housemother!"

Ellie blinked as her eyes made out the figure of Mrs Hall standing there in the doorway in her dressing gown.

"Uh-oh," muttered Naomi.

"You might very well say 'uh-oh'," Mrs Hall snapped. She strode further into the dorm. "And what's all this food doing in here? You know the rules! No food in dorms! In the bin with it all, please, right now!"

Guiltily the girls picked up their goodies and started putting them in the bin.

"Now back to bed, all of you," Mrs Hall ordered sternly. "We'll talk about this in the morning. Don't let me hear another peep from any of you, or you'll be in even more trouble!"

There was a glum silence after she'd left.

"Ouch," whispered Ellie. "I guess we were too noisy, huh?"

"I didn't even get to eat my apple pie," Naomi whispered grumpily.

"Well, you can blame yourself for that," Lara said from her bed. "You and your ghost story!"

The following morning, all of the Year 7 girls felt tired and grouchy. Nobody had slept very well after Naomi's spooky story. Ellie had dreamed all night that she was being chased through the halls of The Royal Ballet School by a ghostly Mrs Hall. The other girls complained of similar nightmares.

Mrs Hall visited the dorm after breakfast. "As you know, girls, it's Final Audition day today for next year's intake to The Royal Ballet School," she said. "And the candidates, of course, will be given a tour of this dorm."

She folded her arms across her chest, a stern expression on her face. "I'll be bringing in a dustpan and brush, so that you can make sure every last crumb from last night is swept up. Then I'm taking you all on a trip to Sheen, to be out of the way of the auditions."

Naomi made a silly face as Mrs Hall left the room. "Anyone would think she didn't get a good night's sleep last night, she's in such a bad mood," she joked.

Ellie rolled her eyes and grinned, and then turned to make her bed, and tidy up the photo frames on her chest of drawers. Afterwards, she helped Lara and Bryony with the huge banner they were making.

When Ellie had come to White Lodge for her own audition a year ago, she'd loved seeing the Year 7 girls' dorm, with the "Good Luck!" banners that the girls had put up for the auditionees. "I can't believe a whole year has passed since our auditions," she said, kneeling down next to her friends as they coloured in the letters together.

"A whole year since we met, Ellie," Lara said with a grin.

Ellie laughed. "Don't remind me," she groaned.

Ellie's final audition hadn't gone very well. She'd misjudged her position in a set piece and, as a result, had crashed straight into Lara. Lara had been so mad about what she'd thought was a deliberate act of sabotage that she'd held a grudge against Ellie through the start of the school year. It was a relief to Ellie that they could both laugh about it now. At the time, it had seemed like a complete disaster!

Grace was pulling on her coat. She was going home for the weekend. "Sorry I can't help," she apologized. "Mum will be here in a minute. Have a good weekend, all of you!"

"Bye, Grace," Ellie called. "There! Finished."

They pinned up the banner, which read

Good Luck In Your Auditions! and then, once Mrs Hall had come to inspect the dorm, the girls hurried downstairs to get the school minibus to Sheen.

Dear Diary,

I've just had some awesome news! Mum called and she said that the musical Fame is coming to the West End, and would I like to go for a birthday treat in a few weeks? YESSSS! How cool will that be? She said she'll book tickets for me, her and Steve for a matinee the Saturday before my actual birthday. When I told the others, Naomi joked that she was going to smuggle herself into my mum's handbag and come too. "If I'm thinking of applying to a performing arts school, I need to do my research, don't I?" she said. I can't wait to go — talk about a treat!

It was funny coming back to school today after our trip to Sheen, knowing that lots of girls had been looking around our dorm, hoping and praying that they did well enough at the audition to be sleeping here themselves come the new school year in September. I remember the tour of the school really clearly but I was feeling so miserable by then because I thought I'd blown my chances after crashing into Lara. I could hardly bear to look at our lovely dorm.

I wonder who'll be sleeping in this bed in September? It's a strange thought.

I'm feeling very sleepy tonight after being up late at our party last night — even if it didn't go on for very long. Everybody else from our dorm is in bed already, all set for an early night. I just can't stop yawning! Going to catch some zzzs now — can't keep my eyes open!

Chapter Eight

The following Thursday, Naomi's parents came down to The Royal Ballet School for the day, and Naomi was excused from lessons that afternoon for a meeting with them, Miss Purvis and Ms Bell.

"I'm missing English, chemistry and French," Naomi said happily, gathering up her brochures after lunch. "What a shame!" She winked.

Ellie and the others grinned, as Mr and Mrs Crawford exchanged amused glances. "No wonder you were pleased when we said it'd be a Thursday we were coming down," Mrs Crawford joked. "And I thought you were just looking forward to seeing *us* again!"

Naomi laughed and linked an arm through her mum's. "Of course I am," she said. "You've just got impeccable timing, that's all, Mum. And speaking of timing, we'd better get a move on," she said. "Don't want to be late for our meeting!" She held her brochures tightly with her free arm and giggled. "Wait until you see Ms Bell's face when I tell her I've actually *read* these brochures now. I think she was really starting to worry about me!"

"Good afternoon, everyone," said Ms Swaisland, their English teacher, as Ellie and her friends filed into her classroom. "I want us to do some creative writing today." She chalked up some words on the blackboard:

FLIGHT OF FANCY

"This is the title of today's writing assignment," she announced. "Does anybody know what this phrase means?"

Kate put her hand up. "Is it like a daydream, Ms Swaisland?" she asked.

Ms Swaisland nodded. "Pretty much," she said. "My dictionary describes it as a 'soaring mental journey beyond the everyday world'. It's a form of escapism, mentally taking yourself away from humdrum everyday life." She smiled around the classroom. "Not that life here at The Royal Ballet School could possibly be humdrum for any of you, I know," she went on, "but I want you to take that as your starting point. Come up with a character, either imaginary or somebody you know. It could even be yourself. Then I want you to write about this character's flight of fancy. It could be anything – let's say an English teacher's secret dream to travel around South America, for example," she said. "If it's someone imaginary, be creative. If it's something personal, write about something you aspire to do, your particular favourite daydream. OK? And there's no need to rush to get this done. You can finish it as your prep tonight."

Ellie thought hard. "What are you going to write about?" she whispered to Grace.

Grace smiled rather sheepishly. "Me, as a world-famous choreographer, putting on a sell-out new ballet," she said.

Ellie raised her eyebrows. "Not *dancing* in the sell-out new ballet?" she asked.

Grace smiled. "That's my *second* flight of fancy," she said. "I've got more than one, you know!"

"Don't forget to start off by describing where your character is before he or she goes off on the daydream journey," Ms Swaisland instructed. "Then I'd like to know what causes your character to escape to his or her fantasy. Does a certain sight or sound or smell trigger a memory? Or does somebody say something, a crucial phrase, which takes your character away from his or her surroundings and into their private thoughts?"

Ellie picked up her pen and started to write a story about a grandmother who, whenever she heard a certain piece of music playing, was transported back to her days as a soloist in The Royal Ballet. By day, the grandmother lived an ordinary life – minding her grand-children after school, baking cookies, and weeding her garden. But every evening, she'd put on a CD of classical music, rest her tired old legs on the couch, close her eyes, and take a flight of fancy back to the days when she was fit and supple, and could spin across the stage in a blur of *pirouettes*.

Ellie's own legs twitched under the desk as she wrote about the grandmother's gnarled old feet. She couldn't help wondering what *she'd* dream about when she was an old woman. Would her legs still be able to remember the way they had once stretched into a graceful *arabesque*, or carried her across the floor in a series of *temps levés*? Would she be able to show her own grandchildren photographs and mementoes of her time as a professional dancer? Oh, she hoped so!

I guess I won't know for a while, she thought, writing furiously. *I guess none of us know what the future holds*. She looked over at Naomi, who was chewing her pen and gazing thoughtfully into space. *Least of all our Naomi, who doesn't even know yet where she'll be next year!* Ellie thought, sighing to herself.

That evening, Ellie and some of the other girls were talking about their writing assignment in the common room when Naomi came in, bursting with news.

"I've decided!" she announced dramatically.

"Decided what, you crazy girl?" Ellie asked, grinning.

"What I'm going to do next year, of course!"

Naomi grinned back. "I want to go to a performing arts school."

"Oh, Naomi! That's great!" Ellie was so happy to hear that Naomi finally knew what she wanted to do.

"That sounds so perfect for you, Naomi!" Grace said.

"Yes, I'm going to apply to three schools – in Manchester, Birmingham and Edinburgh," Naomi told them. "They all seem to have really fab programmes, and my parents like the sound of them, too," she added happily.

"Will you have to do anything when you visit?" asked Bryony.

"I don't think so," Naomi replied. "Apparently, a recommendation from The Royal Ballet School will be a great intro-duction for anywhere! How cool is that? Once I've been to the schools and chosen which one I like best, I stand a good chance of get-ting a place there!"

"So what's the next step?" asked Lara.

"Well, Miss Purvis will telephone each school to arrange a visit for me and my parents," Naomi replied. "So, I'll be on my first national tour over the next couple of weeks – Manchester, Birmingham and Edinburgh here I come!"

"Well, I hope you don't start touring next weekend," Ellie joked back. "Otherwise you'll miss my twelfth birthday celebrations!"

"And it wouldn't be a party without a Madame Naomi astro-reading!" said Kate.

The girls had already planned some small festivities in the common room for everyone who was staying that weekend, and, of course, Ellie had *Fame* to look forward to.

"I wouldn't miss it for the world," said Naomi cheerfully, giving Ellie a hug.

Ellie hadn't seen her mum and Steve since the half-term vacation, so she was really looking forward to spending time with them. However, on the Friday night, Ellie's mum called with a slight change of plan. "I'm sorry, honey, but Steve's come down with the flu," she said. "And he doesn't want to annoy everyone in the theatre by coughing right through the performance. So there's a spare ticket. Do you want to ask one of your friends to come, instead?"

Ellie was just about to call across to Grace and ask her if she'd like to come, when she saw Naomi singing a funny, made-up song into her hairbrush and reducing the others to tears of laughter. "I know just the person," she said, smiling. "Thanks, Mum. Tell Steve I hope he feels better, and I'll see you tomorrow."

Ellie clicked her mobile off and waited until Naomi had finished her song and then went over. "Naomi? There's something I need to ask you," she said, trying to look as solemn as possible.

"Ask away," Naomi said, looking surprised. "What is it?"

"I don't suppose there's any chance you have the time tomorrow afternoon for a trip to see *Fame* with me and my mum?" Ellie asked, grinning.

Naomi's mouth fell open so wide she nearly swallowed her hairbrush microphone. "You're serious?" she gasped, a smile breaking over her face.

Ellie nodded. "I'm serious," she said. "Well? Is that a yes?"

Naomi beamed. "Yes, PLEASE!" she cried, throwing her arms around Ellie. "Yaaaaayyyy! *Fame*, here I come!"

"Surprise, Ellie!"

"We've gatecrashed your birthday trip!"

The very next morning, it was Ellie's turn to have her mouth fall open in surprise. For there, grinning cheerfully at her from the back of her mum's car, were her friends from Oxford, Phoebe and Bethany!

"Happy Birthday!" they both shouted, grinning from ear to ear.

Her mum was smiling at her from behind the wheel. "Hi, sweetheart," she said, opening the car door and stepping out to give Ellie a hug. "I picked up a couple of hitch-hikers on the way," she joked.

"Oh, thanks, Mum!" Ellie cried, delighted to see her friends from home. "Hi guys! What a cool surprise! Pheebs, Bethany, this is Naomi."

"Hello," Naomi said, smiling at them. "I've heard a lot about you two!"

Ellie and Naomi got into the car and then Ellie's mum drove them into Richmond, where they took the train into central London.

"This is going to be so brilliant, I just know it," Naomi said, bouncing around in her seat and unable to stop smiling. "Don't take this the wrong way, Mrs Brown, but I'm so pleased your husband got the flu!"

Naomi was right; the show was amazing. Utterly spectacular! Ellie, her mum, and her friends all sat transfixed as the performers sang and danced their way through the story.

"Wow," sighed Naomi afterwards, as they wolfed a pizza in a cosy Italian restaurant. "I just want to go to *that* school, and be a kid from *Fame*!"

"What, and leave The Royal Ballet School?" Bethany asked incredulously. She had auditioned for a place at The Royal Ballet School herself but unfortunately hadn't been selected.

Ellie winced. She hadn't got a chance to tell her friends not to mention school life in front of Naomi. She didn't want to make a big drama out of it, but she didn't want Naomi to feel hurt or embarrassed either.

Naomi cut herself another slice of pizza. "I *am* leaving The Royal Ballet School," she said, with a rueful smile. "Unfortunately. I didn't make it through the appraisal last month."

Bethany turned bright red and looked very uncomfortable. "Oops. Sorry," she said. "I didn't know."

"That's OK," Naomi said easily. "Honestly. It was a killer at first, but I've kind of got my head around the whole thing now. I really *had* already decided to apply to performing arts schools," she told Bethany and Phoebe. "Shame the one in *Fame* is fictional!"

"I think I'll join you," said Bethany with a dreamy look on her face. "All that dancing and singing. . ."

"Not for me, girls," Ellie grinned. "It was truly amazing, but all I want to do is ballet!"

"Oh, yes! If Ellie sticks with ballet, it will at least keep her from singing – not her strong point!" joked Naomi.

136

Phoebe giggled. "I'm the only person at this table with two left feet, and while we were in the theatre, even *I* was dreaming of studying there."

"It's what our English teacher would call a total flight of fancy," Ellie said with a smile, and then she grabbed Naomi's arm as an idea struck her. "Hey! How about that for your choreo title, Naomi? Flight of Fancy!"

Naomi's face lit up. "Flight of Fancy," she mused. "I like that." She cocked her head on one side. "*Flight of Fancy*, directed by Naomi Crawford. Yeah, I really like that. I think I've got my title! Thanks, Ellie!"

"Don't thank me, thank Ms Swaisland," Ellie replied. She turned to explain to the others, who were looking confused. "Naomi needed a title for her entry in the Junior Choreographic Competition. She's been trying to think of one for ages, haven't you, Naomi?"

"For ever," Naomi agreed. "But now, thanks to the brilliant Ms Brown here and, of course, our beloved English teacher, Ms Swaisland – I'm sorted!" She grinned. "Ms Swaisland, I am forever in your debt," she went on in a melodramatic voice. "How can I ever repay you? I'll do anything. Anything!"

Ellie grinned at her friend. "Doing your English homework might be a start," she said. "Remember? It's due in on Monday. Our final draft of *Flight of Fancy*."

Naomi rolled her eyes. "OK, when I said I'd do *anything*, I didn't mean that sort of any-thing," she laughed. "Oh, all right. As it's Ms Swaisland, I suppose I'd better. And it *is* a good title!"

The others were all laughing. "Celebrations all round," Mrs Brown said cheerfully. "Speaking of which, perhaps it's time our nearly-birthday girl opened presents. What do you say?"

"Yes, please!" Ellie said at once, with a grin. "Today is just getting better and better!"

Bethany had brought her a sparkly little purse and Phoebe gave her a bracelet-making kit.

Ellie ran around the table to hug them both. "Thank you so much! You guys are the best!"

Ellie and Naomi all but danced their way back into school that evening. It had been such a wonderful day.

Naomi hugged Bethany and Phoebe good-bye when Mrs Brown dropped them off. "I feel like I've made two lovely new friends," she said happily.

"Good luck with your search for a performing arts school," Bethany said, hugging her back warmly. "I hope you find one as cool as the one in *Fame*!".

Phoebe grinned at Naomi. "And I'll look forward to your West End stage debut, Naomi," she said. "And good luck with *Flight of Fancy*!"

"Cheers," Naomi said, then threw her arms around Ellie's mum's neck. "Thank you so much for taking me," she said. "I've had a lovely time."

"My pleasure," Mrs Brown laughed. "Now where's my girl? Come here for a birthday hug."

Ellie squeezed her mum tightly as they stood outside White Lodge together. "Thanks, Mum," she said. "That was such a treat. And thanks for asking Bethany and Pheebs, too. Very sneaky of you – but I'm so glad you did!"

Ellie hugged her friends goodbye and she and Naomi waved and waved until Mrs Brown's car had disappeared into the twilit haze of Richmond Park. "I just don't want this day to end," Ellie said, wrapping her arms around herself with a small shiver.

"Ahh, but it's your birthday tomorrow, isn't it?" Naomi reminded her. "And that'll be another great day – you wait and see!"

* * *

"Happy birthday!" the girls chorused after belting out a round of "Happy Birthday" for Ellie, led by Naomi.

Ellie blew out the twelve candles on the delicious-smelling double chocolate cake her friends had ordered from the school kitchen for her.

"Make a wish!" Naomi reminded her.

Ellie squeezed her eyes shut. *I wish . . . I wish I'll be at The Royal Ballet School for my birthday next year*, she thought to herself. *And the year after that, and the year after that . . . oh, for as many years as possible, please!*

It had been a gorgeous day. She'd had a choreo rehearsal with both Grace's team and Naomi's, a long phone call from Heather in Chicago, and now a special birthday cake and presents in the common room.

Grace gave her a hairband and some pretty sparkly clips, Bryony had chosen a new book that had just come out, Kate gave her some warm pink and yellow socks, Lara gave Ellie a CD and Belle had asked a friend in Paris to send over some of the delicious French chocolates she knew Ellie loved.

Ellie was so happy to be surrounded by so many friends. "Thanks, guys," she said. "These are all so lovely."

"And here's mine," Naomi said, handing over a spectacularly wrapped present with an enormous gold ribbon tied around it.

Ellie undid the ribbon carefully and opened the paper. "Oh!" she cried at once.

"Ugly bunch, aren't they?" Naomi joked.

"What is it?" Lara asked.

Ellie held it up to show them. Naomi had framed a photo of all seven friends – Ellie, Lara, Grace, Naomi, Bryony, Kate and Belle. Ellie vaguely remembered Naomi's mum taking it for Naomi at the end of the previous term. The seven of them were all bouncing on

Naomi's bed together, laughing and waving.

"This is so great, Naomi," Ellie said softly, looking at all of the happy faces in the picture.

"I've got a matching print for everyone," Naomi announced, handing out a copy of the photograph to each girl.

"Cheers, Naomi!" said Lara and Bryony together, both looking delighted.

"Oh, Naomi, you shouldn't have!" said Kate, clearly touched.

"Yes, thank you," grinned Belle. "I'm going to keep this for ever."

"Me too," said Grace. "I'll treasure it!"

"And for the birthday girl, there's this, too," Naomi added, handing Ellie a card.

Ellie opened up the birthday card to find a personal horoscope that "Madame Naomi" had written for her. She started to read it, then burst out laughing. "Listen up," she said, and read it aloud.

Hey, Aries! You're in for a fabulous year! Not only will you be in a winning team for the school choreography competition, but you will also be talent-spotted by The Royal Ballet and asked to dance a solo in their Christmas show! A Hollywood movie director will then ask you to star in the latest blockbuster movie – with three Hollywood studs no less – and overnight you'll become an international superstar. You'll even get to understudy Ms Naomi Crawford in The Sound of Music in the West End!! Oh, but you still won't be able to sing. Sorry!

Ellie threw her arms around Naomi, still chuckling. "Thanks, Madame Naomi," she said, and then hugged her other friends, too. "Thanks, all of you. You know, even if my horoscope *doesn't* come true—"

"Of course it will!" Naomi exclaimed, sounding offended. "Serious stuff, astrology, you know!"

"Oh, I'm sure it will, but just on the

off-chance it doesn't," Ellie giggled, "I still feel like the luckiest girl alive. You guys are the best!"

"Oh, we know," Lara said, smirking. "You don't need to tell us that, Ellie."

"And just you make the most of this niceness," Grace added, wagging a finger jokily, "because for the rest of the term, Naomi and I are both planning to work you to the bone in order to win the choreo competition!"

Dear Diary,

I meant it earlier when I said I felt like the luckiest girl alive. I've had such an amazing birthday weekend! I'm writing this in my new pjs (from Mum) with my new hair clips in (from Grace), munching the last of my chocolates (from Belle). It's official — birthdays surrounded by your best friends are awesome!!

Chapter Nine

Grace and Naomi weren't joking about working Ellie to the bone in preparation for the choreo competition. They had both arranged a gruelling schedule of rehearsals, which meant that Ellie had less free time than ever.

Having started out so well, Naomi's piece ran into problems when Kate came down with a terrible cold. She refused to pull out of Naomi's choreography, but she was unable to dance for long without needing to blow her nose! Ellie was impressed by her determination.

However, Naomi got off lightly compared to Grace. In Thursday's weekly gymnastics class, Belle, who was usually so graceful and footsure, fell awkwardly as she was coming off the vault, and twisted her ankle. "Ow!" she cried, tears of pain gathering in her eyes. "I can't move my foot!"

The gymnastics teacher, Ms Johnson, rushed over at once and carefully examined Belle's ankle. Already, Ellie could see the skin swelling up around Belle's ankle joint where she'd twisted it.

Ms Johnson gently pressed the swollen area and Belle cried out in agony. "It's a nasty twist, I'm afraid," Ms Johnson said. "Could one of you run and ask the school nurse to come, please? Tell her we've got an ankle injury."

Belle's face was ashen, as Megan obediently ran from the room. "Might it just be a bruise?" she asked desperately, her eyes flicking over to where Grace was standing. "I'm dancing in the choreography competition."

Ms Johnson looked doubtful. "I'm not sure

you'll be doing any dancing for a little while, Belle," she said gently.

The school nurse came in a few minutes later. "Nothing broken," she diagnosed. "Just a twist – but it does look sore," she added sympathetically as she carefully strapped up Belle's ankle. "Now, let's get you up as painlessly as we can," she said. "Lean on me, that's right, I've got you," she said, helping Belle up. "I'm afraid you're going to need a crutch to get around for the next few weeks. You mustn't put any weight on this ankle until it's completely better, OK?"

"No dancing?" Belle asked in horror.

"Absolutely none whatsoever, until I say so," the nurse said in a voice that meant business. "Now, I want you to elevate that ankle to counteract the swelling."

Belle looked as if she was about to cry as she was led out of the room. "Sorry, Grace," she said mournfully. "I am so sorry!"

Grace's face was equally stricken. "What

am I going to do?" she asked Ellie, her eyes never leaving Belle's departing figure. "I've lost one of my dancers! How will I be able to do my piece now?"

"Could *you* dance in place of Belle?" Ellie suggested. "After all, who knows the routine better than you?"

Grace shook her head. "No! No way!" she cried. "It's stressful enough, just choreographing the thing," she confessed. "I'll go to pieces if I have to dance as well, in front of the judges." She sighed anxiously. "But who else could do it? So many of the girls are already dancing in Naomi's piece."

Ellie racked her brains for a helpful suggestion, and then her eyes fell upon Matt, who was doing a back-bend at the far end of the gymnasium. Since his own piece had been knocked out in the first round, Matt had played no further part in the choreography competition.

"Would it have to be a girl who replaced Belle?" she asked thoughtfully. "Because I know a boy who really wanted to be a part of the competition."

"Who?" Grace asked, with a bit of hope entering her voice.

"Matt," Ellie said. "He might be interested in dancing for you, Grace."

Grace looked over to Matt who was still arched over in his graceful back-bend. "Do you know, that's not a bad idea," she said slowly. "Ellie Brown, you're a genius!"

At supper that evening, Grace and Ellie cornered Matt while he was eating a mouthful of hamburger.

"Hi, Matt," Grace began. "I know this is a bit last minute, and I know you probably have a million other things to do, but I was really hoping you'd want to dance in my piece for the choreo competition."

Matt swallowed his mouthful and said, "But . . . will there be enough time for me to learn the choreography?"

"We can teach you the routine starting tonight," Ellie put in. "Belle's going to help, too."

A huge grin broke out on Matt's face. "I'd love to!" he said. He hugged Grace across the canteen table. "Hey, does that mean I get to dress up in a mermaid costume?"

Grace giggled, relieved that he'd said yes. "Luckily for you, I haven't seen the wardrobe mistress yet, otherwise you'd be squeezing into Belle's costume! But I've got an appointment with her tomorrow, so I'll ask if you can be a merman," she went on.

"Maybe we could get you a long wig and a trident, too," Ellie added.

Matt pretended to cuff her, but he was smiling as he turned to Grace. "Grace, for you, I'll wear anything you want," he said. "Now, when's my first rehearsal?"

Naomi wasn't finding her last weeks of rehearsals to be all plain sailing either. In addition to the exhausting schedule she'd set herself and her dancers, she had her own costume meeting with the wardrobe mistress to attend, and she was also travelling up and down the country with her parents, visiting the three schools she liked best.

"Mum's desperate for me to come back to Manchester," Naomi told her friends with a grin after she'd been there, "and it does look like a really fantastic school. Plus I'd get to see my old friends again, which would be good. But. . ." She shrugged. "Honestly, I don't know what's got into Mum. She's been all mushy about wanting to have me nearer to her and Dad. I can't understand it! She's never like that, usually."

Now all Naomi had to do was choose which school she liked best, but she was finding that to be a tough decision. According to her, *all* of the schools looked brilliant. "It's too much, having the choreo competition *and* a massive life choice like this at the same time," she wailed to her friends. "I keep changing my mind!"

"Consult your crystal ball, Madame Naomi," Lara advised her. "See what the stars recommend."

Naomi just looked more stressed at the suggestion. "I did try that, but even my astrology book hasn't helped me this time," she complained. "I'm just going to have to make up my mind all by myself, aren't I?"

Ellie nodded. "It looks like you are," she said giving her shoulders a supportive squeeze.

Dear Diary,
Things are getting tense now that the choreo competition is drawing near. I know Grace isn't sleeping very well, even though Matt is

proving to be an absolute star, never putting a foot wrong, etc. He's picked up the routine as easily as if he's been dancing it for weeks. Grace is stressing about the smallest details, though – the sequins on the costumes being the wrong colour and how to do mine and Bryony's hair... Bryony, meanwhile, has got Kate's cold, and she's sniffing and coughing in a very un-mermaid-ish style but is dancing on, like a trouper. Poor Grace. She's going to be sooo glad when this is all over next week.

Naomi, on the other hand, is freaking out because her piece is coming in way too long. The maximum time she's allowed is three minutes, but Flight of Fancy is running at almost four and a half! It's a shame she has to cut any of it out because it's all so good, but I guess that's another decision she'll have to make.

There are only three days left until the

competition itself. I can't believe the term is almost over already! All I can do now is practise, practise, practise, and hope that I dance my best for both Grace and Naomi. They deserve nothing less!

Chapter Ten

"It's competition day, everybody! Wake up!"

Ellie opened her eyes at Naomi's voice and was instantly awake. Competition day – finally! She'd lain there half-dreaming about it for hours, going over that tricky section in Grace's choreography where she, Bryony and Matt had to *pirouette* together. And when she hadn't been dreaming about Grace's piece, it had been Naomi's. She'd tapped her feet under her covers as, in her head, she'd danced her way through the most recent, shortened version of Naomi's choreography.

Now, Ellie just hoped she didn't get the two

dances confused while she performed! She looked over at the neighbouring bed, where Grace was lying quite still, staring up at the ceiling. "Grace, did you get any sleep?" she asked.

"I'm not sure," Grace replied, yawning. "I think so. But it took me for ever to drift off. I kept imagining everything in my choreography going wrong, over and over again, in this horrible, inescapable loop!"

Ellie swung her legs out of bed. "In a few hours, it'll all be over," she reminded her friend. "And tonight all you'll be dreaming about is the gracious acceptance speech you gave when you won!"

"Hey!" Naomi called out, sounding affronted. "I heard that! I hope you aren't taking sides over there, Ellie Brown!"

Ellie tickled one of Naomi's feet as she walked past her bed on the way to the shower room. "Of course not, Naomi," she said. "I'm confidently predicting there'll be *joint* winners of this year's choreography competition – you *and* Grace."

"That's more like it," Naomi said, putting on her dressing gown and following Ellie to the shower room. "Fingers crossed, everybody!"

The choreo competition was set to take place that afternoon. It seemed like the longest morning ever to Ellie. Usually she loved her ballet class with Ms Wells, but today she had a paranoid Grace breathing down her neck, whispering, "Careful, Ellie!" every time she attempted a difficult movement. It wasn't exactly the most helpful accompaniment to her concentration.

"Grace, quit saying that!" she groaned in annoyance after the fourth or fifth time. "You're really distracting me!"

"Sorry," Grace said, "but I'd just *die* if you got yourself injured now. Seriously, I think I'd just fall on the floor and die." She shut her eyes and shuddered. "I just hope Matt isn't doing anything silly in *his* ballet lesson," she went on fervently. "What would I do if another of my dancers hurt themselves?"

"Don't worry so much, Grace!" Ellie said firmly. "It's not as if we want to get injured! And you know, you whispering at me and being paranoid is just going to make *me* worry about it and not concentrate!"

Grace looked even more nervous at the idea. "I never thought of that," she said. "Sorry, Ellie. I'll leave you alone, I promise."

Despite her promise, though, Ellie could still feel Grace's anxious gaze upon her for the whole class. It was truly a relief to get her sweatpants on when Ms Wells announced that the lesson was over.

"Now, Grace, do you trust me to climb the stairs back to the dorm without injuring myself?" Ellie joked as they left the studio. "Or maybe I should ask somebody to carry me?"

Grace coloured slightly, and she looked sheepish. "I know, I know!" she wailed. "I'm a worrier and a fusspot. I just so badly want to win; I couldn't bear it if anything went wrong now."

"Nothing's going to go wrong, Grace," Ellie said. "Take some deep breaths. We've got the whole of art class now to get through, and lunch, before it all starts. You're going to collapse with the stress before then if you don't chill a little!"

"In, out, in, out," teased Lara, passing them on the stairs.

"Shake it all about," Naomi giggled. "You do the hokey-cokey and you turn around. . ."

Finally, Grace managed a smile. "Maybe I should scrap *Mermaid's Dream*," she joked. "Ellie, do you think you, Bryony and Matt could do the hokey-cokey as my competition entry instead? Then I might be able to stop worrying!"

Up in the dorm, Naomi's mobile was ringing. She ran over and snatched it up. "Hello?" she asked breathlessly. "Oh, hi, Mum. Yes, I *am* sitting down," she said sounding a little concerned, hurriedly sitting down on her bed. "Why? What is it?"

The other girls stood around, trying not to eavesdrop too obviously. It was clear that Naomi's mum was calling with some important news.

"It's done? It's all arranged?" Naomi squealed. "Oh, YES! YES! Brilliant news, Mum! Oh, I'm so pleased! Did they phone you this morning?"

Ellie grinned across at Grace. It was *good* important news, that much was clear.

"Oh, thanks, Mum. I'm so thrilled," Naomi was saying. She was jumping around now, doing thumbs-up signs to them all, and beaming. "I've got to tell the girls! They're all staring at me as if I've gone mad." She listened for a second and grinned. "Good luck? Mum, after what you've just told me, I'm on a roll. This is a lucky day all round!"

She hung up and threw herself on her bed, squealing and kicking her legs around. "Manchester said yes! I've got a place, and it's all sorted out! They phoned Mum up this morning and told her!"

"That's great!" Ellie cried, rushing over to hug her friend. "I didn't even know you'd made your decision!"

Naomi blushed. "I didn't want to tell anybody, just in case it all went pear-shaped again," she said. "Even though Miss Purvis kept saying that I would get a place, coming from The Royal Ballet School, it just seemed too good to be true. So for once in my life, I managed to keep my decision secret until

I was sure it would all work out. But now I can tell you all, because they've definitely given me a place there. Yippeee!"

"Fantastic!" Ellie said warmly.

The rest of the dorm echoed her. "Well done, Naomi! Well done!"

At long last, it was time for the dancers and the choreographers to make their way to the large Margot Fonteyn Studio, ready for the choreography competition. The seats were full of guests, staff and students who weren't competing. The three judges were Lydia Pelham, who had been a Principal with The Royal Ballet some years ago, Sarah Cross, soloist with English National Ballet, and, of course, the celebrity judge choreographer currently with Birmingham Royal Ballet, Jonathan Wright.

Ellie could feel her heart pounding as she pulled on her mermaid costume – an aquamarine leotard, with a full skirt of glimmering sequinned material that represented the mermaid tail. Bryony had, thank goodness, managed to shake off her cold. They took it in turns to curl each other's hair into ringlets with Naomi's curling iron, and then Grace dusted blue and silver glitter all over their faces. Matt was wearing an aquamarine unitard that covered his whole body, legs included, and they all had glitter on their ballet shoes.

Grace's piece was first in the competition, followed by Nick's, and then Naomi's.

"OK, you can do this, I know you can, you all look fantastic, please keep thinking swirling underwater thoughts and calm, calm, calm. . ." Grace babbled just before they went on.

Ellie actually felt quite relieved when Grace was called to the wings to prepare for her announcement. There was far more calm,

calm, calm once Ellie, Bryony and Matt were left to get on with the dancing, without their worried choreographer fussing over them!

Grace announced her ballet and then went to sit beside the Ballet Principal to watch as the dancers got into position and Ellie took a deep breath. *Here goes!* she thought to herself, waiting for the familiar sound of the waves to begin.

It didn't. All that could be heard was the reels of the tape going round.

"Oh, no . . . I must have forgotten to rewind!" Ellie heard Grace gasp. Blushing wildly, Grace looked up at the box – the technical room at the back of the studio, where all the lights and sound were operated.

Ellie looked too, and could see the boys doing the sound hunched over the controls in there as the silence continued. She tried not to be distracted. *Focus, focus, calm, calm, calm . . .* she told herself. At last, she heard the rushing sound of waves on a beach that was her cue. They were off!

Ellie forgot all about dancing in front of the judges, and let the music flow through her body as she went into the opening *port de bras* sequence of the dance. She tried to make the movements of her arms as smooth and elegant as possible while keeping her lower body completely still. She was glad Grace had coached the three of them so thoroughly; she almost felt as if she could dance the steps in her sleep now. And although she was concentrating hard on exactly what she was doing, she could see that Matt and Bryony were both dancing exquisitely, putting in perfect performances.

Before she knew it, she was spinning to an end once, twice, and then Ellie's ears were ringing with the sound of applause from the audience, the judges and the other contestants.

She, Bryony and Matt held their final

position for another few seconds as Grace joined them for a final bow before coming off stage.

"Well done – well done! You were all wonderful," Grace whispered to them. She shook her head. "It was me who blew it, messing up the music like that. Thank goodness the guys figured it out quickly and put it right!"

Ellie laughed. "Grace, only you could think that a teeny-weeny detail like that would go against you," she said, drinking some cool water thirstily. "It's over now. You did it! You can just enjoy the rest of the show."

Unlike me, she thought, rushing over to get changed for Naomi's piece. For her routine, Naomi had got all of the girls plum-coloured leotards with silver beads stitched around the neckline, and short silver skirts.

As a finishing touch, the costume mistress had found wigs for all of the girls. Lara was delighted with her Marilyn Monroe style wig, and Ellie was excited about her mass of dark curls. Kate looked the most different in her red wig, but she seemed to be enjoying it. The boys wore suits and bowler hats and carried canes.

"We all look so fabulously glamorous!" Naomi whispered once they were all ready. She peeped through the glass pane of the studio door. "Nick's piece is just finishing. We're on, Team Crawford. We are ON!"

Naomi's enthusiasm was infectious, Ellie thought, smiling to herself, as they went on stage and got into their opening positions. Nobody could possibly feel nervous with Naomi there. They were all too excited at finally being able to show the judges what they could do. Naomi wasn't a nervous person anyway, but even with the pressure of the competition weighing upon her, the good news she'd received that morning had her riding on a wave of happiness and optimism.

Nothing could possibly go wrong in her eyes!

"Sock it to 'em, guys," Naomi whispered, as the opening bars of music started. "And smile!"

The brassy, uplifting notes of the tune Naomi had chosen rang out around the studio, and the dance began. There had been so many last-minute changes and cuts to the routine that Ellie's biggest worry had been that she'd get confused. But with Naomi counting out the beats – "One, two, three, and *pas de chat, pas de chat*" – throughout, it was a simple matter of tuning in to her instructions whenever Ellie felt any doubt.

There was a huge round of applause at the end, and Ellie couldn't help beaming as she put her arm on Justin's shoulder in the final position.

Naomi stepped forward and gave a cheeky curtsey, and was rewarded by cheers from the audience.

Ellie couldn't help smiling at her friend. She just brought such enthusiasm to everyone around her! And this performing arts school was going to be just perfect for her; Ellie knew it. Naomi would be totally in her element!

"Well done, everyone! Thank you for working so hard," Naomi cried as her dancers came off stage. "Lara, fabulous jumping. Kate, I just loved that wink you gave the judges at the end. Sassy mama! Ellie, brilliant timing all the way through. All of you were superstars. I mean it!"

Ellie was hit by a wall of exhaustion. All that work, and now it was over! She could hardly believe it. What an exciting competition!

"Come on," Lara said. "Let's go and watch the others dance now."

"That," said Ellie, grinning, "is the best suggestion I've heard in a long time."

* * *

There were three competition entries from Year 8. Somehow Ellie appreciated the dances even more, knowing from personal experience just how much time and effort each one would have taken to practise and perfect.

Martin's piece was called *Daffodil* and was a solo piece danced by Natasha who had painted her face yellow and wore a petal headdress and green body stocking. She skipped and *jetéd*, looking every inch a daffodil blowing in the wind.

Then came Jason's piece, in stark contrast to Martin's, called *Disaster*. Ellie thought it was very brave to use such a large cast of dancers. Eight boys leaped in *grands jetés* to dramatic music, whilst eight girls lunged, *pirouetted* and *bourréed* amongst them creating a sense of frenetic chaos.

The next piece, *Nightfall*, began with a Year 8 couple dancing joyfully, and then the lights dimmed and they slowed down with the music. The dancers went to "sleep" and dream spirits rushed in to dance around the sleeping couple, their costumes floating in the breeze making them look like shadowy spirits.

After the last piece had finished, there was a performance by some of the older dancers to entertain the audience while the judges went out to deliberate. But Ellie could hardly concentrate on them; she was too busy wondering what the judges were saying.

As the performance came to a close, Grace and Naomi had grabbed each other's hands.

"Good luck," Naomi said.

"Same to you," Grace replied, then made a strangled sort of noise as if something had got stuck in her throat.

Ellie looked up to see The Royal Ballet School's Director, Lynette Shelton, coming to stand at the front of the studio, with a smile on her face.

"I hope you all enjoyed watching the

competition entries as much as we have," she said. "The standard has been extremely high this year. Well done to all of you. And now, to announce the winners, I shall hand you over to Jonathan Wright."

There was a round of applause as the young choreographer stepped forward, clapping for the choreographers and dancers. And then the room fell silent once more.

"It is always difficult to pick out winners from such a varied mix of styles and dancing. We were particularly impressed by the way so many of you used and expressed the themes and musicality of your soundtracks," Jonathan went on. "But, after much deliberation, the results, in reverse order, are as follows: in third place with *Nightfall* . . . Carli Taylor!"

Ellie clapped as hard as she could for Carli, the friendly, talented girl from Year 8. Ellie was especially pleased because Jessica, her guide from Year 8, had danced in the piece.

"In second place, with *Daffodil* was Martin Weekes," Jonathan said, to a rousing cheer from a group of Year 8 boys. "Well done, Martin." He paused, as Martin came up to stand next to him and Carli.

"Which leads me on to the announcement of the first prize," he went on, when the clapping had died down. "All three of us judges were unanimous in our decision. The winning piece of choreography was well-crafted, ambitious and, frankly, a joy to watch. We were very impressed by the way this choreographer used their piece of music to influence the movements of the dancing, and the visual patterns that were created."

He smiled. "I won't keep you in suspense any longer. The first prize in this year's Junior Choreography Competition goes to . . . Grace Tennant for the beautiful *Mermaid's Dream*!"

"Yes!" shouted Ellie, jumping to her feet, applauding her friend. "Grace! You did it!"

"I did it," echoed Grace, looking disbelieving. Then a smile broke over her face. "I did it!"

"Grace, please step forward," Jonathan said, smiling broadly. "A round of applause for Grace Tennant, this year's winner!"

Everyone got to their feet as Grace went up to the front of the studio, looking utterly dazed and overwhelmed. Ellie glanced across at Naomi to see how she was taking the results, but she needn't have worried. Naomi was beaming and cheering Grace as loudly as everybody else, and Ellie felt a great rush of affection for Naomi, who was so generous even in defeat.

"And finally," Jonathan said, "we have a special commendation we'd like to make. There was one piece that particularly impressed us all, with its wonderful showmanship and theatricality. Not only was it great fun to watch, it was also striking in its ambition. Would everyone please put their hands together as we give an honourable mention to the choreographer of that piece, Naomi Crawford, who gave us the fabulous *Flight of Fancy*!"

Now it was Naomi's turn to look dazed, as a huge roar of applause swept around the room.

Ellie felt the hairs stand up on the back of her neck, and an enormous smile spread across her face. "Wow, Naomi!" she squealed. "Fantastic!" She was so, so pleased for her friend. It was wonderful that she was achieving this recognition after the terrible news about her appraisal. To bounce back and put her all into the choreo competition took real courage and strength of character. She'd been right earlier that morning – she hadn't needed any good luck wishes! It was just *her* day.

"Well done, Naomi!" Ellie and her friends

cheered as Naomi went to the front of the studio and curtseyed in front of everybody. The dazed look from Naomi's face vanished rapidly and before long, she was beaming and waving at the audience, and blowing kisses to her friends.

That evening, after showering their tired bodies, Ellie and her friends put on their best dresses and went down to the dining room for supper. It felt fitting to dress up for the occasion, somehow. It had been such a big day! And how strange it was not to be rushing from one rehearsal to the other. Ellie was going to be glad to have some down time from now on.

Naomi had been desperately trying to call home to tell her mum how the competition had gone but she'd had no answer. "I'm just going to have to take my phone into the dining room," she said, stuffing it into her pocket. "I know that's very rude of me, but this is an emergency! I need to boast of my humongous success today!"

The meal began, with everybody tucking hungrily into plates of pasta. There was a choice of salmon linguini or vegetarian cannelloni, plus piles of steaming, fragrant garlic bread and lots of different salads. Ellie's mouth watered. After dancing so hard, she was hungry enough for two dinners!

Before long, Lara was on her feet, a glass of juice in her hand. "I think we should all have a toast to Year 7's superstar choreographers, Grace, Naomi and Nick," she announced to the rest of the table, holding up her glass.

"To Grace, Naomi and Nick!" everybody chorused, clinking glasses.

"Speech!" called out Matt, waving a hunk of garlic bread enthusiastically in the air.

"Oh, no," Grace protested at once, turning red. "Um ... just ... thank you. That's my speech. Thank you to my wonderful dancers – Ellie, Bryony and Matt, and to Belle too, of course. It was you who won the prize really, with your awesome dancing."

"Rubbish!" Matt called out. "Stop being so modest, Grace! It was your brilliant choreography!"

Grace blushed violently, but she was smiling all the same. "I'm just so pleased and excited. I talked to my mum earlier and she was really happy!"

Then, Naomi got to her feet. "Did somebody ask for a speech?" she said, putting a hand to her ear.

Ellie laughed and cheered. "Go on, Naomi!" she called. She should have known Naomi would have had no qualms about getting up and speaking to everybody.

Naomi's face turned serious for once. "Actually, there *are* a few things I'd like to say," she said.

"Now *there's* a surprise," Lara grinned.

Naomi pretended to glare at Lara, but then her expression turned grave once more. "I can't tell you how hard it was, coming back to The Royal Ballet School after being appraised out," she said. She bit her lip at the memory, as if it still hurt her inside. "I was so utterly miserable. It was as if somebody had knocked me over, and I just couldn't get up again." She paused and looked around the table, her eyes soft. "You guys – my friends – were amazing. The support and friendship I've had from all of you has blown me away, honestly. When I came back to school, the last thing I felt like doing was entering the choreo competition. There was no point, I thought. I'll only fail that as well. I might as well give up completely."

Ellie noticed that everybody on the Year 7 table had stopped eating. All eyes were on Naomi.

"But my friends never once gave up on me, or wrote me off," she went on quietly. "I can't tell you what that did for me, knowing that you lot were still rooting for me, helping me with the competition, and encouraging me to look ahead to other good things in my future." She paused for breath. "So I want to say a massive, enormous, gigantic thank you to Ellie, Lara, Kate, Grace, Bryony and Belle in particular. If it wasn't for the six of you, I probably wouldn't have entered the competition, and I certainly wouldn't be here, tucking into a celebration dinner!"

Ellie found that she had tears in her eyes and, looking around the table, so had Kate and Grace.

"Well, thanks to all your work, you are," Lara reminded Naomi. "You deserve all this, Naomi."

Naomi pretended to look modest at the compliment. "Aww ... shucks," she said, mock-bashfully. Then she grinned and put her hands on her hips. "Right, well, that's enough of the serious stuff for one evening," she said. "I'd like to make a toast to the Year 7 girls' dorm: plenty more triumphs for us all!"

"CHEERS!" everybody bellowed.

"And the boys' dorm, too," Justin put in quickly.

Suddenly, the theme music from *Fame* filled the air.

"I recognize that tune!" said Ellie grinning.

"Yup, it's my new ringtone," beamed Naomi, pulling out her phone. "Hi, Mum!" she said happily, sitting down. "Where have you been? I've been ringing you for ages!" Her face turned serious. "Oh. Is everything OK? You're not ill, are you?"

Ellie couldn't help overhearing, even though she didn't want to eavesdrop. She nibbled at her garlic bread anxiously, hoping Naomi wasn't receiving bad news.

But Naomi was suddenly all smiles again. "No!" she was gasping into the phone. "No way! Is this a joke? Wow. WOW! I can't believe it! That is so exciting!" Her eyes were bright as she drank in whatever her mum was telling her. "Oh, Mum, that's so lovely. That's so... What? My news? Oh, it hardly compares! I got an honourable mention in tonight's competition. They really liked my routine! But ... wait ... can I call you back after supper? I've just got to tell everybody *your* news first!"

She clicked off the phone and sat there, with a strange expression on her face.

"What? What now?" Lara begged. "You look like the cat that got the cream, Naomi. What's happened?"

Naomi's face was alight with happiness. "I'm going to be a big sister again!" she cried. "Mum's having another baby! She said she had her suspicions for a few weeks but didn't want to say anything until she'd been checked out by the doctor, but it's really happening!"

"And you're going to be at home in Manchester, too," Ellie said. "You were so meant to go to that school, Naomi!"

Naomi grinned. "You know, I did wonder why Mum kept going on about how nice it would be for me to be back home," she said, winding some linguini around her fork. "That must have been what she was thinking of!"

"I think we'd better have another toast," Grace said, holding her glass up in the air. "To baby Crawford!"

Lara got to her feet again, brandishing her glass. "Here's to baby Crawford, *and* to Naomi, *and* to Manchester!"

"To Naomi!" echoed Ellie, smiling across the table at her friend.

"To Naomi!" everyone cheered at once.

Naomi clinked glasses with everybody sitting around the table, looking happier than she had done for weeks, and Ellie couldn't help feeling that it was the perfect ending to what had been a truly memorable second term at The Royal Ballet School. It had been tough at times, and certainly challenging for all of her friends. But with Grace winning the choreography competition and Naomi's future looking a good deal brighter than it had done at the start of this half-term, things were really looking up once more. And who, thought Ellie, sipping her juice happily, could want for more than that?

Dear Diary,

I can't believe I'm packing to go home for Easter already. This term has flown by, and, boy, has it been a roller coaster ride! What with the excitement of passing my assessment – but then the devastation of finding out that Naomi would be leaving us at the end of the year. I can't bear to think that next term is going to be the last few weeks we'll have with her – but I know we'll all make the most of her while we've still got her. And at least we know she'll be going to a fantastic new school near her new baby brother or sister.

Grace was so thrilled to win the choreography competition – especially as her mum said she was really proud of her and sent her a big bunch of flowers.

And I'm more determined than ever to do my very best to stay at The Royal Ballet School for the whole programme and become a professional ballerina!

But one step at a time – my first summer term here at The Royal Ballet School comes next. I wonder what that will be like? I just can't wait to find out!